Ghost Stories Ink presents

NIGHT VISIONS

Edited by Jessica Freeburg & Natalie Fowler

RED SOFA BOOKS
St. Paul, MN

Copyright © 2015 by Ghost Stories Ink

All rights reserved. No part of this publication may be reproduced, distributed or transmitted in any form or by any means, including photocopying, recording, or other electronic or mechanical methods, without the prior written permission of the publisher, except in the case of brief quotations embodied in critical reviews and certain other noncommercial uses permitted by copyright law. For permission requests, write to the publisher, addressed at the address below.

RED SOFA BOOKS
PO Box 40482
St. Paul, MN 55104
www.redsofabooks.com

Publisher's Note: This is a work of fiction. Names, characters, places, and incidents are a product of the author's imagination. Locales and public names are sometimes used for atmospheric purposes. Any resemblance to actual people, living or dead, or to businesses, companies, events, institutions, or locales is completely coincidental.

Book Layout ©2013 BookDesignTemplates.com
Cover Design by Shawn McCann

Ordering Information:
Quantity sales. Special discounts are available on quantity purchases by corporations, associations, and others. Distributed by Itasca Books.

NIGHT VISIONS/ Ghost Stories Ink -- 1st ed.
ISBN 978-0-9912456-3-5

For our families and friends, who support us in our creative endeavors. And for Tristin, who taught us how to be ghost hunters.

With love,
Ghost Stories Ink Crew

INTRODUCTION

Ghost Stories Ink (GSI) was born at the Palmer House Hotel in Sauk Centre, Minnesota in January of 2013, after I coordinated a ghost hunt for myself and any brave friends who wanted to join me. Several of those friends were children's authors and illustrators (including GSI founding members Shawn McCann, Scott Spinks, and Sean Spinks). Afterwards, I couldn't shake the idea that we needed to form an official group of kid lit creators who'd perform paranormal investigations for creative inspiration. The idea kept me awake at night; finally I gave in to the wee-small voice in the back of my head and reached out to Shawn, Scott, and Sean about creating the group behind the anthology you're reading today.

My vision for Ghost Stories Ink was simply for our adventures to inspire our creative works. I never imagined the friendships we would form along the way. GSI has become a small family that supports each other creatively and personally. I often joke I've brought together the strangest children's writers and illustrators group ever. The truth is that I simply planted a seed. Together we have made it grow into what it has become today and into the future.

While we still perform investigations with our core group, our mission has evolved from just inspiring ourselves to also inspiring others. We began offering writing and illustrating workshops in the basement of the Palmer House. Surprised by the number of people who began showing up, we realized this is a creative niche we can have fun filling.

Our retreats offer others the opportunity to allow history to speak to them directly and through them creatively. I'm humbled by the number of people who attend our workshops, and I'm excited to hear about each of their projects and dreams as writers and artists. I am honored that Ghost Stories Ink could be even a small part of their author/illustrator journeys. I'm also thrilled to open up our anthology to include a couple of stories from our workshop/retreat participants.

As I worked through the edits on the stories in this book, I teared up several times. Not because I was so scared that I cried – although these stories are creepy enough for such a reaction. I was honestly overwhelmed by pride for what each of these authors created. And I was touched by the realization that Ghost Stories Ink brought these stories out of the writers in NIGHT VISIONS.

I hope you will have as much fun reading these stories as we had writing them. If we're lucky, one day you will join us on an adventure. Maybe you have a story sleeping inside of you that is just waiting to be awakened by a good, creepy ghost hunt.

—Jessica Freeburg, Founder of Ghost Stories Ink

REPEATED

By Jessica Freeburg, Founder of Ghost Stories Ink
Inspired by the Palmer House Hotel

The car jolted to a stop, sending Beth slamming into the metal frame of the backseat. Her wrists had been tied behind her back for so long that the pain in her shoulders had gone from excruciating to complete numbness. When she'd been stuffed into the trunk, the musty smell of dirty gym socks and wet carpet made her gag. Eventually she had become accustomed to the stench.

As the car sped along, she felt it travel from paved roads to gravel, then back to blacktop, possibly a highway. Oddly the car stopped a time or two – perhaps at an intersection. Beth assumed someone traveling with an unwilling passenger in their trunk would be sure to come to a full stop at all stop signs.

She tried to scream, hoping they were in town; but the gag around her mouth made her voice crawl back into her throat. It was unlikely she was in her town, where her captor nabbed from her behind as she walked to her car from the mall. She had been just a few steps from the 1963 cherry red, Ford Falcon her farther had gifted three months ago on her sixteenth birthday. Some girls loved fashion. Beth had instead inherited her father's love for cool cars, of which he was all too happy to give her a great set of wheels for her birthday, as long as he could "test drive" it periodically to make sure it was running okay.

The mistake was the inadvertent digging in her purse for the Falcon's keys. She remembered her mother's voice, "Always be alert in a parking lot. Have your keys out before you leave the store." If only she had kept her head up, maybe she wouldn't have been such an easy target. A tear slipped down her cheek, only to be absorbed by the rag tied around her mouth.

When the trunk popped open, the dull light of the street lamps against the night sky made Beth squeeze her eyes shut. Even the subtle light was an explosion of brightness after being in the tar black of the car trunk's traveling prison. As the man threw her over his shoulder, she frantically kicked at his torso. One shoe had flown off in his battle to get her into the trunk. She prayed the police would find it and know she had not just run away. Her parents would know she hadn't, but wasn't that always the first thought the law enforcement had when a teenager went missing?

The large buckle on the man's leather belt met the flesh of Beth's bare foot with a sickening crack. She winced at the pain and tilted her head from one side to another, trying to get a sense of where she was. The man carried her swiftly through a back ally. On one side, a towering structure composed of bricks darkened with the dirt of age. On the other, a smaller structure with faded wooden steps leading up to a metal door.

In a few speedy footsteps, the man was at a back entrance using Beth's backside to push through the cold door, entering the taller of the two buildings. As she strained to see where he was taking her, the side of her head smacked against the doorframe. Her eyes blurred with tears as the man carried her through a large commercial kitchen. What remained of the appliances appeared to be out of date. A refrigerator door, ripped from its hinges, rested against a large metal table heaped with bits of crumbled plaster that had fallen from the ceiling above.

Slamming through a set of double doors, Beth watched the tile floor change to faded wooden planks. As the man turned a corner, she read the word "Hotel" printed in chipped paint on a dirty window. She craned her head, which was throbbing from a combination of fear and the blow to her head. Soon the banister of a staircase appeared, and the man plodded up the steps, grunting under her weight. She squirmed whenever possible, refusing to make it easy for him.

The stairs creaked with each footfall. They continued upwards, past a landing where a broken bench flanked the wall, up another set of steps and down a long hallway. The only light peeked through a cracked window at the far end of the corridor. The same dull glow of street lamps Beth had seen when the trunk was opened. After two more flights of stairs, they seemed to reach her captor's intended destination. He stumbled on the last few steps, clearly exhausted from carrying Beth's one hundred and ten pounds of wiggling weight up two stories.

The man grunted as he pushed a door open. A busted headboard rested against one wall where a bed likely once stood. A single wing-back chair stood in one corner, nearly obscured by the shadows. The man entered the dark, musty room and heaved Beth's body onto a tile floor. Her head smacked against something hard and cold on the way down. She felt the warmth of blood roll down her neck as she winced her eyes in pain.

The stale scent of tobacco wafted into her nose, as the man leaned all too close to her. The wet, warmth of his breath against her cheek caused her to press her body further into the wall he had thrown her against.

"Please don't hurt me," Beth whimpered, her eyes still closed, as if not seeing the evil in front of her might make it disappear.

"I don't want to hurt you," he rasped back. "I only want to watch you die . . ."

He wrapped his hands around her throat and squeezed. Beth opened her eyes. His face was so close to hers that she could only see the darkness of his eyes and the bushy, black eyebrows that arched above them. His nose was nearly touching her own. His jagged, excited breaths puffed against her lips.

Beth's head began to pulse and her lungs ached as she became deprived of oxygen.

Her vision blurred and everything faded to black.

His words echoed faintly in the distance. " . . .but not yet," he grumbled. Her limp body dropped back against the wall.

Beth held her breath as she listened for any sign that the man might be in the room before using one hand to slide the chain around the pipe from the corner of the bathroom wall up to the base of the sink. She moved the plastic zip tie that secured her wrist to the chain a fraction of an inch toward her hand. Just enough for her to see the bloody line around her wrist she had created by trying to pull it off. She had abandoned any hope of that when she saw the blood dripping down her arm. For a moment, she worried she may have accidentally slit her wrist with the tie. She'd found a certain satisfaction in the idea that she could die from a self-inflicted wound. At least then she wouldn't give that sick bastard the satisfaction of doing it himself.

NIGHT VISIONS

He had attached her to the pipe while she was unconscious. She thought he had killed her, like he said he was going to. She felt a twinge of disappointment when she'd woken up, but it was quickly replaced with a determination to survive.

The chain prevented her from standing up completely. She straightened her legs, but her back remained hunched, causing her ligaments to stretch painfully. Beth had very little sense of time, but she could hear music playing from somewhere in the hotel. She tried to stand and stretch her legs every couple songs. If she sat too long, her legs would completely fall asleep, and she wanted to be ready to run if she ever got the chance.

That music, it was as if it came from a different time. It reminded Beth of the music she'd heard in a western movie she'd once watched with her father. The thought of her father made her choke on a sob. He would never get over losing her. She had to get out of this somehow and get home to her parents.

NIGHT VISIONS

She settled back onto the floor and closed her eyes, allowing the tears to warm her cheeks.

"He'll be coming soon," a voice whispered from somewhere across the room. Beth had not seen her unlucky roommate. She had only heard her speak a few times. She knew her name was Lucy, although she wasn't certain when the girl had introduced herself.

"Why is he doing this?" Beth whimpered, more to herself than to the other girl.

"I've seen him do it many times. It never ends well . . ." Lucy's voice trailed off on the last word.

Beth pulled her knees to her chest. The darkness of the room was nearly blinding. The small window across the room had been covered with a torn sheet that blocked out most of the streetlight's illumination.

Wiping away her tears with her one free hand, she crouched again, this time not to keep the circulation going to her feet, but to get closer to the sink.

"I'm not going to let him kill me," she said, running her free hand along the pipe. Starting at the wall, she slowly moved up to the base of the sink. Just before metal met porcelain, she felt a ring. Using the hand tied to the pipe, she grasped the pipe below the ring, and with the other hand she grabbed the pipe above. She pushed and pulled, trying desperately to pull the pipes apart.

"They've rusted together," Lucy whispered.

Beth continued pulling and pushing on the pipe. "There has to be a way."

The sound of the door creaking open made Beth freeze.

"He's back." Lucy's voice was tight with urgency.

Heavy footsteps crossed the room. Soon the man stood above her, his face twisted into a maniacal smile. Beth began frantically pulling at the pipe again. Her eyes, wide with terror, darted from the man, to the pipe and then back to the man. She kicked at him wildly – one shoe still on, the other somewhere in the parking lot that now seemed a lifetime away.

Then it happened - the pipe miraculously pulled away from the wall. She slid the chain down over the rounded, metal cap that had secured the pipe to the wall. Her hand still bound by the zip tie that had been fastened through a link in the chain.

Beth swung her arms in front of her body, whipping the man in the face with the metal link that had bound her to the sink. He cried out and stumbled back as she scrambled to her feet and rushed past him.

She felt his hands wrap around her ankle as she ran, causing her to careen forward. She tried to break her fall by grabbing at the sheet crudely hung from nails above the window in front of her. She pulled it down with her, letting the dull light of the street lamps below brighten the darkness of the room before her face smacked into the windowpane. Blood immediately gushed from her nose.

The man was on her before she could push herself up from the floor. He rolled her over and straddled her body, putting his weight on her stomach, pinning her helplessly to the floor. His hands once again wrapped around her throat. Blood trailed from his forehead where the chain had made contact with his face, dripping from his chin. His eyes, rimmed with ashen circles, were dark and cold. An evil smile split his mouth, revealing crooked teeth, yellowed from the tar of cigarettes.

As her senses were swallowed into the darkness of the man's death grip, Beth saw the girl, standing just behind him. Her dress was from another time, like the music Beth had heard – she looked as if she had stepped out of a black and white photo from the 1800s. Lucy seemed to flicker, and for a moment, Beth could see right through her.

"Take my hand." Lucy's voice seemed to wrap Beth like a warm blanket, as her body began to tremble until it became still. Beth felt herself being pulled away from her motionless body.

She stood beside the girl, both of them looking down at her lifeless form, pinned beneath the man.

"Am I dead?" Beth asked, her voice shaking, afraid she already knew the answer.

"Yes," Lucy replied.

"Are you dead?"

"I have been for many years." She put a hand on Beth's shoulder, which seemed strange to Beth that she could feel a touch on her shoulder as she looked down at her own dead body. "You have been dead for many years, as well."

"What?" Beth asked, a new wave of panic washing over her. "No, I'm right there! He just killed me!" Beth pointed toward the floor. "He murdered me, right there!"

Only instead of her body, she saw a small suitcase opened on a foldable rack positioned under the window. The window, where she had moments before ripped the grungy sheet from a rusted nail, was now dressed in wooden blinds and a pale blue valance.

Beth spun around, looking into the bedroom. The busted headboard that had rested against the wall was replaced with a large mattress framed by ornate, antique wooden posts. A man and woman sat on the bed, their eyes darting around the room.

"What was that?" the woman asked, her voice tight with fear.

"I don't know," the man replied. He cleared the cobwebs of sleepiness from his throat as he grabbed the phone on the nightstand. "Yes, this is room 17. We cannot sleep in this room," he said firmly into the receiver. "I know you warned us, but the pipes in the bathroom have been banging all night, and now we just heard a terrible crash against the wall."

The woman hurried toward the window. She walked through Beth and Lucy on her way to the suitcase. Beth gasped. The woman spun around her eyes searching the space around her.

"Did you hear that?" she asked, her voice nearing hysterics as she looked through Lucy and Beth, completely unaware at them looking back at her.

"She walked through my body," Beth said in awe.

"Your body has been gone for a long time, Beth," Lucy said gently. "Only your spirit remains."

"It's freezing over here!" the woman exclaimed with a shiver as she zipped the suitcase shut. Pulling it off the rack, she hurried toward the door and slipped on her shoes.

"Aren't you going to get out of your pajamas?" the man asked.

"No!" she shrieked. "We're getting out of here, right now!"

The pair rushed from the room, the door slamming shut behind them.

Beth stared at the door in shock.

Lucy's hand remained on her shoulder, she gently used her other hand to brush a stray strand of hair away from Beth's face. "It's alright, dear. This happens every year on the anniversary of your death."

Her voice was calm and motherly. "It happens to all of us. We just slip back to that time for a few moments."

Beth began to calm down. She was beginning to remember. Lucy had stood beside her last year, in this very spot, saying these same words.

"That man killed me . . ." she said, her words hung in the air for a moment like a bubble waiting to pop. Lucy stood beside her and nodded sadly.

The door squeaked open and a woman walked into the room. She adjusted a pair of glasses on the brim of her nose as she looked around for a moment, before walking toward the television and snatching a set of car keys.

"Kelley. . ." Beth whispered.

Lucy rubbed Beth's should gently. "You're remembering, now."

"Well, it looks like you did it again," Kelley spoke into the air with a slight grin. "I tried to warn them. This room always seems to be most active this time of year, but they insisted. Thrill seekers. Well I guess you gave them what they came for." She jingled the keys in the palm of her hand. "Ran out of here so fast, they left their car keys."

She walked toward the door, put her hand on the knob and paused. Turning to face the room Kelley said, "I'm not sure what it is about this time of year that gets you so riled up. I tell ya' what, I'll keep this room closed the next day or two. Let you have your space a bit."

"Thank you," Lucy's voice floated across the room. It was anyone's guess if Kelley could hear it. Maybe she could sense it, like she always seemed to do.

Her smile widened. "You look out for me. Call me crazy, but I can feel it. You deserve that much from me in return."

The door shut gently behind Kelley as she left.

The two spirits moved across the room and sat on the bed together, Lucy's arm wrapped protectively around Beth's shoulder. "It's hard to come back after repeating those final moments of life," she said calmly. "But give it a little time, you'll be okay, my dear."

Beth nodded quietly.

"It's not fair the way you came to be here, but it's a good place to be, none the less."

Music wafted under the door. A soft, gentle melody that made Beth smile. "The gramophone," she said.

"She knows that music makes us happy," Lucy said.

"Let's go listen," Beth said.

"Everyone will come out for the music. Are you sure you're up to it?"

"Music is good for the soul. That's what my dad always said," Beth smiled, remembering her father.

"Very well, then," Lucy brushed the wrinkles from her skirt as she stood. "I'm always in the mood for music."

Together, the two passed through the wall leaving the room empty. The laughter of the dead gathered in the lobby to enjoy the music, reverberated down the hallway. Despite death, this was a happy place. And the souls made the most of the joy that filled the space where they had lived, and where some had died. Their joys and pains had become echoes. Sometimes noticed. Sometimes unnoticed. But always there, endlessly.

THE LAST SUPPER CLUB

By Jay Asher
New York Times Best Selling Author
Friend of Ghost Stories Ink
Inspired by El Coyote

Connor waits for the red dome atop the studio camera to glow. Two years ago, they were using his girlfriend's handheld smartphone, recording and editing in his dad's kitchen. They would post a twenty to thirty-minute show online for anyone to watch at any time. The most basic graphics. No music.

Now, it has become a thing. A rising star on the pop culture scene. Ninety minutes to two hours long, each meal's preparation unfolds in real time around pre-taped interviews and photo slideshows that play while meat cooks or vegetables steam. The cooking itself is all done live, instantly streaming to thousands once that red light blinks on. Most watch it for the slow reveal of crime details and the personalities behind the true and gruesome stories, but the real eeriness comes from knowing a significant number of other viewers are cooking right along with Connor.

Sick bastards.

The red light flashes on. Standing beside the camera, originally purchased solely for the school's morning video announcements, Maddie points to Connor, who finishes tying his "Don't Kill the Cook" apron. He looks through the tilted plate of glass in front of the camera lens where bright green words scroll upward, invisible to the audience. The first words, like his closing words, are the same every month.

"Welcome...to The Last Supper Club." He gracefully lowers the backs of his hands to the classroom's kitchen countertop, imagining himself as Jesus at the original Last Supper. Two thousand years ago, they ate roasted lamb, hardboiled eggs, and bitter herbs like any good Jew at Passover. Tonight, those who dine with The Last Supper Club will repeat another historic meal.

Outside, only two protesters have shown up. One holds the same sign that has been here ever since production moved to the high school six months ago: "Kill the show, not our school's reputation!" It began with forty protesters. After those protesters were interviewed on local news, twice that number showed up at the next recording. When national news picked up the story, the number of protestors tripled, but viewers shot up thirteen thousand times.

Lynn's glass of wine sits near a printed out list of ingredients and cooking instruments for tonight's feast. Based on the complexity, she's fairly certain it's a death row inmate's last meal. Those meals make up a quarter of the episodes on The Last Supper Club. Unless someone is coming home from a night at a fancy restaurant, most people don't have apple chutney, arugula, and spices that are only available at specialty stores in their stomachs when they die.

From a propped up tablet, Connor speaks directly to Lynn. "Thank you for joining us as we, once again, taste the dark side of humanity. With a dash of psychology and a dollop of history, we'll experience a tragedy together."

Lynn kicks her head back to drink the last drop of her first glass of wine. The glass clinks as she sets it on the counter again, and then she pours herself another.

Ms. Duvall rinses her hands in a classroom sink next door, having spent two hours scratching interlocking diamonds onto the ceramic jug she's been working on this week. Her students spent their week on vases made by rolling strands of clay, bending each strand into a ring, and then scoring and stacking one ring atop another.

The vases were heated and are now cooling in the brick kiln outside. The kiln sits in the center of an open courtyard surrounded by the backdoors to other rooms in the Art and Home Ec. building. Those doors only open when students need to lay paintings out to dry or someone burnt a dish they were preparing and had to air out the room. That happened last month during an afterhours recording of The Last Supper Club. Ms. Duvall never watches the show, but she knew it was their episode on the Charles Manson murders. It may be hard to mess up chile relleno, but they had managed. The teachers complained that their rooms smelled like burnt tortillas for a week.

While she doesn't watch The Last Supper Club, Ms. Duvall is partly responsible for it being shot on campus. In that way, she's responsible for the remaining two protesters outside. Maybe next month, she hopes, that number will dwindle to none.

NIGHT VISIONS

The show used the teacher's kitchen counter, and a wide mirror hung above, angled so students can watch what's happening from their desks. Before each episode of The Last Supper Club, a small camera is mounted to the mirror's edge for the same purpose with online viewers.

Connor lays a sprig of lavender atop the whipped cream in a mixing bowl and then theatrically kisses his closed fingertips. "Perfection! I'm guessing we'll hardly taste the lavender, but if that's what the deceased wanted, that's what the deceased got. And that's what you get."

Maddie jabs her finger toward the scrolling words on the camera. She hates when he goes off script.

Behind her, sitting in a student desk, wearing headphones and staring at the laptop, Sarah smiles at the improvisation.

Connor reads the words prepared for him. "As you find a place in your fridge to let the whipped cream cool, listen as Dr. Solvitz describes what could lead otherwise intelligent people to follow such a twisted fella."

The red light on the camera goes out and Connor turns to the computer on the teacher's desk, which is connected to the live stream. Dr. Solvitz, sitting in a low lit room backed by shelves of books, explains the unmet needs that could leave a person open to the suggestions of a charismatic leader who does not have their best interests in mind.

Maddie turns to Sarah. "How are we doing?"

Sarah runs a finger across the laptop screen. "Not as good as last week, but—"

"Damn it!" Maddie unlocks the wheels of the camera's tripod and rolls it forward a few inches. After every cutaway, Connor's image gets a little closer to the camera—closer to the viewer—and becomes a little more personal.

Connor slides the bowl of whipped cream into the classroom refrigerator, empty except for two cartons of eggs and a stick of wrapped butter. At one of the sinks lining the walls, one of eight student kitchens, he washes his hands so the teacher's sink stays clean for the camera. "Fewer viewers, but we made a lot more money this month."

"More than any month," Sarah says. "But we could make a ton more. We just need to find one murder—really famous—with a fancy schmancy meal and we'll be rolling in it. But they don't watch when no one's heard of the victim."

"Like one of those chefs who have their own cooking show," Connor says. "I bet they eat the most expensive stuff at home!"

"Exactly," Sarah says. "One of them dies and we've got the fame and the fancy."

Connor returns to his post. "Maybe we use the money from this episode to hire someone whose sole job is to find murders we can make money from."

He looks at Maddie, expecting a response. Any time he brings up adding another person to the team, she shoots him down. She insists on choosing and researching the crimes. She only brought on Sarah when the technological side of the show proved too complicated to monitor while working the camera.

Maddie locks the wheels on the tri-pod and then looks over her shoulder at Sarah. "Ready the script."

Connor breathes in and then slowly exhales. The red light comes on and his lines begin to scroll. On the side computer, Dr. Stolvitz blurs and then it cuts to Connor.

"Cults are creepy," he says.

Maddie motions for him to raise his hand.

Connor enthusiastically puts his hand in the air. "Who wants to join one?"

Connor and Maddie hadn't considered the show anything but a fun project that already fit their fascinations. Maddie had been obsessed with murder ever since she brought her parents' true crime book collection, without permission, for her sixth grade Hobby & Craft Fair. The parental uproar made her finally open a few of the books to see what the fuss was about. She was hooked. Last year, she read about a man who killed his wife after preparing an extravagant meal for her. It was part of his months-long apology mission, and also the first time he'd cooked for her. Not only was her legitimate anger unchanged, she complained about every bite. So he strangled her.

The book included the recipe he had followed, and that was when Maddie got her big idea. Since Connor would do anything to spend more time with her, he agreed to help.

They found murders with easy meals and recorded those shows on Maddie's phone to test the interest. It felt as if there were people waiting online for something like this from the beginning. Five months in, they finally prepared the extravagant meal that started it all. Viewership was good that month, but hardly anyone cooked along. Comments leading up to the show, once the ingredients list had been posted, were mostly complaints that people couldn't find one of the spices.

Other viewers directed them to specialty shops, but they either took too long to ship or it cost too much for one shaker of spice. For the next several episodes, they returned to more basic ingredients.

During this time, their school offered a new course in entrepreneurship. Applying for her senior electives, Maddie came up with a way to choose the best murders, even if they had complex recipes, and enrolled in the class to gain access to the school's recording equipment.

Donnallise wipes a damp sponge across the tabletop. From the other room, she hears cupboards banging shut.

"Donny! Tell me you didn't forget to order the spice."

That's Amanda, making an accusation before asking for help.

"It's by the popcorn bags," Donnallise says. She hears the pantry door slide open.

"Got it!"

Donnallise walks into the kitchen to gather plates.

"The meat's almost done," Amanda says, "but I've barely started the dressing."

On the digital screen mounted beneath a cabinet, Connor gives a plastic lemon bottle a squeeze, shooting its juice into a silver bowl.

"Of course, we don't know how many squirts of lemon Daniel would have used, but he did grow up on a citrus farm, so he's probably comfortable with things being on the sour side." He squeezes the lemon one more time.

Amanda opens the refrigerator and pulls out their plastic lemon. She flips open the top with her thumb, closing the refrigerator door with her foot, and then walks to the mixing bowl. After one long squeeze, Donnallise takes it from her and recaps it.

NIGHT VISIONS

"We didn't grow up on a citrus farm."

Amanda picks up the small glass spice bottle pulled from the pantry and twists off the red cap. On the side of the bottle, an oval sticker the color of weathered parchment is imprinted with Old English letters: L.S.C.

"What's it smell like?" Donnallise asks.

Amanda holds it beneath her nose and sniffs. "Hard to say. Maybe some basil cooked in bacon grease."

Donnallise laughs. "You're weird."

"I'm serious!" But now she's laughing as she shakes it into a bowl. Then she stirs the balsamic-based dressing with a wooden spoon.

Ms. Duvall lifts a blade on the dusty mini-blinds to peak outside. One of the protesters either left early or went for a bathroom break. The remaining one puffs on a cigarette.

Sticking around once a month as faculty chaperone for The Last Supper Club gives her time to work on her own ceramics, something she hadn't done in years. But that's not the only reason she agreed to do it.

She walks across the classroom toward the door to the courtyard to check on the projects in the kiln.

Yes a cooking show based around final meals of executed criminals or murder victims was twisted, but the school library had several true crime books. How was this any more exploitative? If these kids were willing to take so much time to research crimes and recipes, seeking interview subjects, recording, editing, and then buying, bottling, and labeling spices to reach the profit goal of entrepreneurship, no one could argue they weren't learning.

She unlatches the heavy bar on the kiln and eases back the door, letting the hot air mix with the cool air outside. After a few seconds, she peeks in. And then she sighs.

Across the layers of shelves, less than half of the vases remain intact. Some student must have accidentally left bubbles in their clay. Maybe several students. When heating up, those pockets of air shattered their clay, and the flying shards became bullets that cracked or destroyed other projects.

At least, she hopes it was an accident.

To mimic the forest around the cabin where today's crime story unfolds, Sarah had gone to the nearby woods and shot footage to play back in slow motion. Last week, Connor recorded himself reading the script Maddie had written for him, which now plays over Sarah's footage.

Sarah laughs, reading comments people are writing in the chat box online. "Some girl took a sip of the salad dressing and said it tastes like vomit."

Maddie leaves the camera and runs to Sarah's computer. "Why did she do that? Everyone's supposed to eat together!"

NIGHT VISIONS

Sarah holds up a hand to keep Maddie from the keyboard. "People already jumped down her throat for that. She hasn't said anything since."

Living in California's agricultural zone, known as America's Salad Bowl, has advantages. Most of their classmates call it boring, but The Last Supper Club sees its richness. With access to hundreds of farms, someone is usually growing anything they need. If a recipe calls for an item out of season in other regions, there's a good chance they'll find enough to satisfy their fans cooking at home. If it's a sprig from an obscure plant, they can get enough cuttings to bag, sticker, and mail it out with enough profit coming back to make the entrepreneur teacher shut up about the show's premise.

Because it's about making money.

If it's a seasoning mix they need, they can find enough of each spice and rent a grinder and mixer by the hour, then bottle, sticker and ship. And since mixes take longer and cost more, the price goes up. The key is finding the most intriguing murder with a hard to find ingredient somewhere within the recipe. Then they record that episode when the ingredient is hardest to find.

They have the supply. They control the demand.

Connor and Sarah often fantasize about a production company being out there somewhere, watching, ready to buy their idea, paying them enough to cover college and maybe a house. But Maddie doesn't care about that.

Connor finishes sending his text and then sets his phone in the utensil drawer and slides it shut. He sees Maddie quickly look from him to the tripod with anger in her eyes as she overly tightens the wheels.

She dumped him three months ago, but when he began dating someone else, it infuriated her. But The Last Supper Club show must go on.

NIGHT VISIONS

Connor pulls the lightly chilled chocolate crème pie from the freezer and places it on the counter.

"Ten seconds!" Maddie calls.

Connor removes the whipped cream bowl from the refrigerator and walks it back to the counter.

Maddie stares right into him as the camera's red light burns.

"It is now time to put our final preparations on this final meal." With a wooden spoon, Connor scoops several heaps of whipped cream onto the pie. He carefully places the empty bowl into the sink. "Keep the main dish warm in the oven and gather around the table. It is time."

Standing outside the view of the camera, Sarah lights a long red candle held in a pewter candleholder. She sets it on the counter a few inches out of the frame.

Connor keeps reading. "It is time to dig in now before someone digs a hole for us . . . six feet deep."

Maddie, managing the final moments of the show, points toward the burning candle. Connor reaches over and slides the candle into frame for ambience.

Sarah returns to her computer desk.

Connor lifts the salad tongs and gives the salad, the dressing, and The Last Supper Club seasoning, one final mix. "So, who's serving?"

Maddie motions for Connor to raise a fork of salad to his mouth. As he chews the customary first bite, Sarah plays the appropriate clip. While viewers enjoy their first taste of this meal, images of the crime's deceased will play across their screens.

In homes across the country, some people sit at dining room tables. Some tables are encircled by groups that get together once a month just for this communal decadence. Or people stand alone in their kitchens, watching with everyone else online. Fraternities. Couples. Even restaurants, two on each coast, have

NIGHT VISIONS

turned their big-screen TVs over to something other than sports.

On the screen, in the same Old English font as the L.S.C. on their spice bottles, it reads: "In memory of . . ."

Connor swallows his first bite. He pushes another forkful into his mouth and watches the monitor off to the side. Maddie often tweaks these clips until the last moment, and this is usually his first time to see the faces of the dead.

"In memory of . . ." fades and a rectangular photo appears of a college student in a baseball cap. But he's too young! Connor looks at Sarah, but she stares at her computer, just as confused.

Another picture appears. A bride and groom kissing.

Sarah screams. "These are our viewers!"

Connor wheezes in a breath. His eyes begin to water with burning tears.

Maddie smiles at him. "Don't worry, I'll do the dishes."

Sarah jumps to her feet, still staring at the computer. "These are profile pictures of our viewers! Maddie . . .?"

Maddie walks toward Connor. With the kitchen counter between them, she leans forward and blows out the candle.

Connor's throat burns as it squeezes tight, a thread of air struggling to reach his lungs. The spice bottle, its lid still open, is gripped in his fist. He wants to throw it at her, but his arm falls against the counter. His knees collapse. He overturns the salad bowl on his way to the hard floor and the spices spill over his chest.

Maddie kneels beside Connor and wipes the hair from his eyes. "You were a great host."

Connor's eyes can't stay focused on the bottle she easily pulls from his fingers.

NIGHT VISIONS

"What we did here today," she says, "this is how we become infamous."

Ms. Duvall sweeps shards of broken clay into a pile on the kiln floor. It's still warm inside its walls, but she's only thinking about what she must tell her students tomorrow. One of their projects blew up the others.

NIGHT VISIONS

3 Darkness Watching

By Natalie Fowler
Historian/Investigator – Ghost Stories Ink
Inspired by the Manor in St. Paul, MN

I skipped around the corner and froze.
There were people in the garden.
We had visitors.
The others will want to know. I hurried off to tell them.

The stone gargoyle perched on the second-story turret sneered a warning, "Don't come in. Stay away." Andi knew it was just her imagination, but it unnerved her just the same. She slammed the car door and wondered for what felt like the millionth time what she was getting herself into.

NIGHT VISIONS

Chaz loved talking about his ghost hunting adventures with his paranormal team. Tonight they would be filming an episode for their YouTube channel. Part of her was flattered he'd asked her to come along, but the other part felt like everything about this night was a bad idea.

She followed Chaz to the back of the car. He pulled out a duffle bag, a camera tripod and spool of electrical cord. Andi swung her tote bag over her shoulder and followed him to the back of the house.

The group was assembling on the back patio. Andi had already met Chaz's roommate, Sam, but was meeting the others for the first time.

"Andi, this is Max," said Chaz as the tall, skinny guy with long, stringy hair stepped forward and shook her hand. "And this is Grant, but we call him Boo."

"Nice to meet you," said Andi shaking hands, trying hard to remember the names.

"We shot our B-roll footage with the homeowner yesterday," said Boo, adjusting his glasses. "He left us full access to the house. We can take a tour in a minute."

I heard their voices outside and peeked out from behind the curtain. *"Miss Tanya!"* I shouted. *"I think they are coming in,"* I said with a giggle.

Miss Tanya floated out through the closet door behind me and peered over my shoulder looking down at the patio.

"Well ain't that a bunch," she chuckled. *"Those boys are just my type."* She looked at me, her black empty eyes staring right through me. *"Did you tell the crabby old man yet?"*

I was the only one who could move around the whole place, so it was my job to let everyone know what was going on.

"No, ma'am," I said. "I came to you first." Miss Tanya liked when I talked to her first.

NIGHT VISIONS

"I'd better go tell him now. He's not going to like it," I said with a sigh, floating toward the stairs to find Harold in the basement. I stayed away from the dark shadows as best I could.

I didn't like to go near the Shadow Thing.

Sam unpacked a video camera. Max was fiddling with gear that Andi didn't recognize. Andi wondered if she could still get out of this ghost hunt tonight, hopefully without disappointing Chaz. She didn't want to embarrass him in front of his friends. Maybe she could fake an illness. Or since she was the only girl, if necessary she could always fake a case of cramps. She swallowed back her smile.

Out of the corner of her eye, Andi thought she saw the upstairs curtain flicker. Her heart beat faster; she willed herself it believe it was just her imagination.

Chaz clapped his hands together; Andi jumped at the noise. "So what do we have here? Where are we starting?" he asked the group.

Boo adjusted his black baseball cap, turning it around so the ghost logo was now facing forward. "We've got a few things going on with this house," he said. He flipped open his tablet and looked over his notes. "The niece of the owner has reported seeing the spirit of a little girl. She was dressed in turn-of-the-century style clothing; she was out in the garden playing when first seen. She's also heard a baby crying."

Despite the warmth of the September night, Andi shivered.

"But that evidence hasn't been corroborated by anyone else. Just the twelve year-old niece," said Boo.

The guys all nodded.

"About twenty years ago, this house was rumored for its debauchery," Boo continued, waggling his eyebrows at the word. "A prostitute known as Tanya was murdered and found in the alley about one block over." He pointed down the street.

Andi shivered again. She reached into her bag for her sweater, glad she'd remembered to bring it.

"I saved the best for last," Boo continued. "The homeowner is in the process of finishing the basement. He wants to make it into an entertainment room. But ever since he began work, he claims the paranormal activity has picked up. He's reported things like tools getting lost or misplaced, and sometimes he feels like someone is watching him."

Sam rolled his eyes. "They always say they feel like someone is watching them."

Max snickered. "And it always seems to happen when someone wants to remodel."

Andi caught Boo's eyes dart to her and then to Max and Sam. "Let's stay professional guys, we have a guest with us tonight."

Max straightened his face. "Sorry," he mumbled.

"Let's sort out the gear and cameras, and get going while we still have daylight to work with. Max, you're in charge of set-up."

Max gave a mock salute. "Yes, sir."

Boo sighed. The group dispersed, each finding a job without talking.

Andi stood next to Chaz who was unrolling his spool of cable. "You never told me I was going to be the only girl," she whispered.

Chaz shrugged, "I didn't know. Everyone always invites their girlfriends. You're the first one to actually show up."

"Mr. Harold," I whispered. My eyes darted to the corner of the basement. The corner where the Shadow Thing often hid. It wasn't there. I almost wished it was. Part of me would rather know where it was.

"What do you want?" grumbled Harold. He turned his back on me and went back to trying to pick up a

brick that was laying in the middle of the room. His wrinkled transparent hand went right through it. Every time.

"*Miss Tanya wanted you to know that we've got company.*"

Harold liked it when other people remembered him, so he gave me his full attention.

"*You don't say?*" His dark eyes flickered with interest. "*Do you think they will come down to the basement?*"

I smiled back at him. "*I'm not sure. Maybe?*"

He answered with a grunt and went back to trying to move his brick. "*Just so long as they don't go moving my workbench all over again. They put it in the wrong place,*" he said looking right through me and pointing to the bench in the other room.

"*I know Mr. Harold,*" I said. I had to listen to him complain about his workbench being in the wrong place every time I came downstairs. I watched him try to pick up the brick.

NIGHT VISIONS

"Can I help you move something Mr. Harold?"

"Nah, thanks anyway, Cora. I've gotta learn how to do it myself."

I nodded.

"But thanks for your help with that bucket of nails," he said. His dark, empty eyes gave me a wink.

I smiled, filled with pride. But then I remembered pride was a sin, and I straightened my face.

"Tell Miss Tanya I said 'thanks'. . .and you can come down and see me any time. It gets lonely down here. And you make good company."

I nodded again. This time remembering to stay serious. *"Just so long as the Shadow Thing isn't here,"* I whispered. *"I don't know how you stay down here with it."*

Harold winked again. *"As long as you stay away from it, it stays away from you. And try not to be afraid, it can smell fear."*

I left, wondering what fear smelled like.

Boo took the lead and unlocked the back door. Sam followed behind, the red light of his video camera signaled that he was recording.

"Andi, why don't I take you on a tour, and Sam you follow and film? We can add it to the B-roll footage. Chaz, you can help Max set up the DVR cameras."

Andi nodded, happy to have something to do. Through the back door, there was a set of stairs that went down to the basement, or up to the kitchen. They headed toward the kitchen. Andi watched as Chaz and Max unpacked a laptop and placed several small cameras and other gadgets on the kitchen table.

"Where do you want us to set up?" Chaz asked Boo.

Max noticed Andi watching him. "This is a K2 meter," he said, turning it on and handing it to her. It was a tool that had a spectrum of lights, from green to red. "It measures electromagnetic energy."

NIGHT VISIONS

Andi just nodded. She could see Sam with his camera out of the corner of her eye and knew he was recording. She didn't want to say anything that would sound dumb.

"And this," he went on, "is a special audio recorder that records EVPs. Sometimes we pick up noises, and sounds, even voices, that we wouldn't otherwise hear with our own ears."

"I think we can make the living room our headquarters," said Boo. "The homeowner said not much has happened in the living room so we probably won't investigate in there anyways."

Andi decided she was going to try to spend as much time in the living room as possible.

"Ok," said Boo winking at Andi. "Where should we start? Upstairs and end with the basement, or downstairs and work our way up?"

Andi shrugged. "Whatever you think," she said trying to keep her voice steady.

"Ok, let's start up and go down," said Boo.

They climbed the spiral staircase that lead to the second floor. Sam and his camera brought up the rear.

"Chaz is really excited you came," whispered Boo. "I've never been able to get any of my girlfriends to tag along on a ghost hunt with us."

"Smart girls," said Andi, her tone flat.

Boo laughed like she'd just told a really funny joke.

Sam reached the last step. "Ok, we're rolling," he said.

"Is anyone here going to come out and play tonight? We came to see you!" Boo shouted into the air.

Andi's eyebrows shot up and she tried not to giggle.

Boo grinned at the camera. "This house went through a substantial remodel in the late sixties, early seventies. It was during this remodel that the groovy spiral staircase was added."

Sam circled the room, ending with a shot looking down over the railing at the spiral staircase.

NIGHT VISIONS

Boo walked through the sitting room to the master bedroom, and over to the closet. "Sometimes," he said opening the door, his voice full of suspense, "this closet door slams all by itself." He slammed the door.

Andi jumped at the noise. Goosebumps raced up her spine and all along her arms to her fingertips.

Sam panned the camera to Andi.

She gave him what she knew was a weak smile.

Boo motioned for Sam to follow him, and they left the room.

Andi glanced at the closed door and followed them. She didn't like being the last one to leave the room. It felt like someone was watching her. Following her.

"Did you see what he just did?" shouted Tanya.

"No Miss Tanya," I said coming through the wall. I only went through the walls when it was an emergency, and by the way Miss Tanya was shouting, this was an emergency.

"*He slammed my door,*" she screeched. "*No one is supposed to slam that door but me. It's all I got! And I can't even do it that often.*"

"*It's ok Miss Tanya,*" I said. "*I'm sure he didn't mean it.*"

"*Oh, he meant it alright,*" she said. "*He'd better just watch out. He said he wants to play; I'll come out and play!*"

I heard the baby crying again.

"*Miss Tanya, the baby's crying, I have to go.*"

"*There ain't no baby crying,*" she said. "*You always say you hear a baby crying. I don't never hear no baby.*"

"*But it is,*" I insisted. "*I have to go. I'll be back.*"

She waved her hand at me, and I hurried off to get the baby.

Andi followed them down the stairs. She still didn't like being the last one to leave, but she took advantage of her moment alone. She stopped on the top step to take

NIGHT VISIONS

a deep breath. She could get through this night, she told herself. Time was a finite resource. At the end of it she would be the only girlfriend brave enough to have gone on a ghost hunt.

"Or stupid enough," she mumbled to herself. She was about to take her first step when she heard it.

It sounded like a baby crying. Somewhere in the house, a baby was crying. A blast of cold air sent shivers down to her toes.

She hurried down the stairs.

"Did you guys just hear that?" she asked, catching up to Boo and Sam at the bottom of the steps.

"No, what?" asked Boo, while Sam pointed the camera in her direction.

Andi looked at the camera and then to Boo, suddenly feeling stupid and wishing she hadn't said anything. "I just thought I heard a baby crying."

Sam moved around and shot up the steps from where she'd just come.

"Upstairs?" asked Boo.

"I don't know," said Andi. She had to concentrate to keep her teeth from chattering. "It was from somewhere in the house. I'm not sure where."

Sam let his camera rest at his side. "It could have been a cat, out in the alley," he said walking to the window that looked out over the backyard. He tapped on the window with a finger. "These panes are pretty thin."

"Or maybe some kids outside," said Boo. "Let's go down to the basement and finish up our tour, so we can get back and help with the DVR set-up."

Andi frowned, but followed them down the steps that led to the old cellar basement.

"Miss Tanya?" I asked, opening the closet door and peering inside. *"Are you ok?"*

She was huddled in the corner, crying.

"What can I do, Miss Tanya? I want to help you."

"I don't like them. I don't want them in our house."

"Is this all because they slammed the door?" I asked.

"My door," she corrected me.

"Sorry, your door," I said working hard not to sound impertinent. Mamma said impertinence was a sin.

"What can I do?" I asked. "How can I help?"

Miss Tanya looked at me through her tears.

"I dumped out a whole bucket of nails in the basement for Harold the other day," I bragged.

She stood up straight and wiped at her face. But there weren't really any tears there. If I didn't know any better, I would have thought she was trying to trick me.

"I think you can help me, Miss Cora. I do think you can," she said with a smile.

"I'll do whatever you ask," I said. "If only you'll stop crying."

"I'll stop crying," she promised.

NIGHT VISIONS

The second Andi's feet stepped off the last step onto the cellar floor, she could feel the change in the atmosphere. "Dude," said Sam from behind the camera. "It feels heavy in here."

The wall along the first room, where they stood held a temporary workbench, fashioned from what appeared to be former kitchen cabinets.

"Yeah," said Boo. "I feel it too."

Andi was quiet. She assumed the change in atmosphere that she felt was what they meant by heavy.

They walked through the workroom into a big, empty room. A single lightbulb hanging from a cord in the middle of the room was the only light, throwing shadows in every corner. The air felt thick.

The dirt floor was uneven and bricks were scattered throughout. Two giant metal beams in the middle of the room seemed to be providing temporary support to the entire foundation of the house.

"I mentioned this place had a few dark years," said Boo catching the attention of the camera. Sam panned towards him.

"Back in the 80's and early 90's, this wasn't the greatest neighborhood and the owner at the time was heavy into drugs. He dealt out of the house and had drug parties in the basement."

Andi shivered. With the new information, her surroundings felt sinister. "I think we should start down here," said Boo. "Maybe all together with a few candles?"

Sam kept the camera rolling but gave him the thumbs up.

"Are you doing ok?" Boo asked Andi.

"Sure," she said, hoping she sounded nonchalant. She felt like the walls were closing in, and she really just wanted to get out of the basement.

I heard footsteps on the stairs. Miss Tanya heard them too. We looked.

"I'm not really sure about all of this," whispered Andi, following Chaz up the spiral stairs. They were almost done with all of the set-up.

Chaz stopped at the top and looked at her. "It will be fine. We do this all of the time; there's nothing to worry about."

Andi wished she could believe him.

"I think you're pretty fine," Miss Tanya hovered behind him and whispered in his ear.

I giggled.

"Where do you want this one?" Chaz asked as Boo came up the steps behind him.

"Let's see if we've got enough cord to get it to the master bedroom, and we can point it at the closet," said Boo.

"The cord," said Miss Tanya looking at me. *"Cora get the cord."* She said, pointing.

I wasn't really sure what a "cord" was. But my hands followed along the thick string she was pointing at until I found a piece that was slack.

"*What should I do with it?*" I asked.

"*I don't know girl, use your imagination. Do I always have to tell you everything?*"

I scowled and studied it. Looping it together I pushed the pieces through each other. I made a nice little knot that would've made my Papa proud.

I grinned at Miss Tanya, and she winked at me.

So long as she's not crying anymore, I'll do whatever she wants, I thought.

I hated when people cried. My Mamma cried. For a really long time.

Andi followed Chaz to the master bedroom, and her heart nearly stopped.

The closet door was open.

"Didn't you," she asked Boo, unable to complete her sentence.

"Didn't I what?" asked Boo.

Andi ignored the hint of impatience she thought she heard in his voice. "Didn't you slam the door shut?"

"Yeah, so?" he asked.

"Well it's open now," she pointed out.

Boo looked at it. "Huh," he said. "Well, probably, someone else opened it."

"I think Max was up here," said Chaz. "He probably opened it."

Andi pinched her lips shut. She was done offering observations.

"Let's get going," said Boo. "This is our last camera, and we've got to get started." He went back downstairs.

Chaz nodded and pulled on the cord. "Hey," he said. "What happened to my cord?"

Andi followed it back towards the stairs until she found the big knot where it had wrapped itself around the leg of the desk.

"Just a minute, you've got a knot here," she said tugging at it.

Chaz came out behind her. "That's quite a knot," he said frowning. "I was careful to make sure they were all out before I started walking around."

Andi shrugged.

I giggled. *"Miss Tanya,"* I said. *"Did you see?"*

Miss Tanya grinned. *"What are y'all doing here tonight?"* she whispered at them while they were trying to work out my knot.

I laughed. I liked to see Miss Tanya having fun.

But I could see she was getting tired. She looked like she was fading away before my eyes.

She knew it too. *"You can do better,"* said Miss Tanya her voice quiet. *"Push them or something. Throw the books."* She pointed at the bookshelf. Her voice was desperate, but almost gone.

I wanted her to laugh, but I would never try to hurt them. I nodded at her with a smile and waited. I watched her fade until she was nothing and went to find Mr. Harold.

Everyone reassembled in the living room. Andi watched the video surveillance screen on the laptop. It showed the four stationary night vision cameras. Nothing was happening in any of the rooms.

"Does it ever catch anything?" she whispered to Chaz.

He shrugged. "Not really, that I've seen," he said. "But this system is new," he was quick to add. "We just started using it."

"Does anyone have any questions before we get started?" asked Boo.

"Do we have any names to work with?" asked Sam.

Boo looked through his iPad notes. "Let's see. We've got the prostitute that was killed near here. Her name was Tanya."

"Yeah, but do we have any names for people who actually lived here?" asked Sam.

NIGHT VISIONS

Boo rolled his eyes. "Didn't you guys read the report I sent?" he asked, looking over his notes.

Max and Sam looked at each other and then down at the ground.

"Do we know if anyone died in the house?" asked Chaz.

Boo sighed. "If you had read my report, you would know that one of the previous owners had a heart attack," said Boo. "His name was Harold, he died here in the early 70's. And the family that built the house in the late 1800's lost two children to a fever epidemic," he said. "A girl, age nine. And a baby."

The hairs on the back of Andi's neck stood on end, and she wrapped her arms around herself to try to stave off the recurring chill that had been haunting her all night.

"How about any Ouija Boards?" asked Sam.

"I'm not sure," said Boo. "The owner said the place was a rental property for about ten years before he bought it, so he didn't know for sure, but it's possible."

Max nodded. "Dude. There are gargoyles guarding the front door. You'd have to be a certain kind of tenant to want to live in this house."

Sam shook his head. "Ouija boards are bad news."

Andi and Chaz had only been dating for three months, so she hadn't known Sam that long. But she knew him long enough to know that he was a guy who would try anything. If he said they were bad, she was inclined to believe him.

"Ok," said Boo. "Let's go down to the basement."

They all filed out of the living room. Andi strategically positioned herself in the middle of the group so she wouldn't have to go first or be the last in line.

Max turned off the center light, and multiple flashlight beams darted around the room revealing the holes in the dirt floor, bricks to watch out for, and cobwebs hanging down from the exposed wood beams overhead. They positioned themselves around the room. Andi watched in horror as the guys all sat right down on the dirt floor. Her flashlight found an empty drywall bucket next to the doorway in the workroom. She claimed it by flipping it over and dusting it off. She was glad she hadn't worn her new jeans.

"Mr. Harold," I asked. "What are they doing?" We stood in the doorway, looking into the empty room. Right behind the pretty girl.

"*I don't rightly know Miss Cora, I don't know. There ain't nothing in there, and they don't have the noisy newfangled machines that they've been using down here.*"

I liked the way Harold talked. And Miss Tanya too. Like they were from another time.

Max struck a match and lit the three candles in the middle of the room. The sulfur from the match filled the room, tickling Andi's nose and was soon replaced by a sweet vanilla scent.

"Seriously?" said Boo. "Who bought scented candles?"

"Max usually smells pretty bad," said Chaz. "I thought it'd be a nice change."

Everyone laughed.

"Ok, let's kill the flashlights," said Boo. The flashlights all clicked off.

"Is there anyone out there who wants to talk to us tonight?" asked Boo. "I've got a special tool that will tell us if you are here." He laid his K2 meter on the ground in the middle of the room. The light of the meter showed that it was on, but nothing happened.

"Who are they talking to?" I whispered to Harold.

"I don't rightly know," he answered. *"Us?"*

"But how do they know we are here?" I asked.

"I don't know," he said. *"I'm downright stumped."*

NIGHT VISIONS

"Here we are, ready to talk to someone! Come talk to us," said Max.

Through the flickering shadows, Andi studied the faces of the ghost hunters. She could see the collective looks of concentration on everyone's faces.

She swallowed back a nervous giggle. Whatever she'd been expecting, having flashbacks to her seventh grade séance slumber parties wasn't on the list.

Chaz shot her a glance.

"Sorry," she mouthed. Andi stared at a spot on the ground and focused on keeping her composure.

"Harold, are you here with us tonight?" asked Sam.

Harold looked at me. *"They said my name! How do they know my name?"*

I giggled. *"I don't know,"* but I thought it was kind of exciting.

But then I saw it.

In the corner. It was watching too.

"*Look,*" I said pointing. "*Shadow Thing is here,*" I whispered.

Shadow Thing was taller than I remembered. It was as tall as the wall, and even had to hunch over a bit. Its eyes were red, its fangs hung out of its mouth, dripping with ooze. I could hear the snorts as it breathed, reminding me of the cows at Grandfather's farm. Its arms were longer than arms should be, and the three fingers on each were more like claws.

"*It's right out of a nightmare,*" I whispered to Harold. Or maybe it was the devil Mama always talked about.

The Shadow Thing looked at us watching it.

"*Shhh,*" he scolded to me without taking his eyes off of it. "*Remember what I said, don't let it see you are afraid.*"

I nodded. Too afraid to say another word.

Shadow Thing looked at each of the people, sitting on the floor. Like he was trying to figure out which to choose for supper.

NIGHT VISIONS

I was worried for them.

But I felt safe by Harold.

Andi felt her body relax. For some reason, for the first time all night, she felt safe where she was sitting, and it was a nice change. Even if she knew it wouldn't last.

I watched the Shadow Thing lurch back and forth. Pacing. It went from one person to the next. Snorting. And smelling.

But Harold was right. It stayed away from us.

"Come on!" said Sam. "Come out and play! We're not afraid of you."

Andi's eyes darted from one face to the next. She wasn't sure if she liked the direction this was taking. What if there was something there? She didn't think they should be yelling at it. Just in case.

I gasped as Shadow Thing jumped over their heads into the center of the circle. Now it turned around. Looking at them. One at a time at each of their faces. Trying to see what? I didn't know.

Maybe Harold was right. Maybe it was trying to smell.

I wanted to hide my eyes. But I couldn't.

Not knowing what happened next would be worse than watching it.

Andi gasped as the candle in the middle went out altogether. At the same time, the K2 meter spiked once, all the way with all of the colors, but then went back to where it was.

The adrenaline pumped through her body and she took short breaths to try to calm herself. But as much as her reflexes made her want to jump up from her spot, something held her in place. That sense of safety she'd felt earlier, she didn't want to risk losing it by moving.

"Dude," said Max. "Did you see that?"

Sam picked up the K2 meter and waved it through the air. It went off near the ceiling.

"There's probably just some piping up there in the ceiling," said Boo.

NIGHT VISIONS

"But the candle went out at the same time," said Chaz.

Boo shrugged. "It could have just been a change in the air flow. Maybe a vent kicked on somewhere?"

"I don't know . . ." said Chaz. "That's kind of a coincidence."

Boo looked around at everyone. "I don't think we're getting much down here. Let's go to a different space, maybe up by the closet?"

Max and Sam nodded.

"Sure," said Chaz. "Whatever you want." He got up from the ground and dusted off his blue jeans.

Andi scrambled up off of her spot. No way was she going to be anything but the first one out of the basement. She took the steps two at a time and headed for the living room with the rest of the group behind.

By the time everyone was reassembled in the living room, Andi's heart rate had returned to normal. She didn't try to hide her yawn.

"Do you guys ever have anyone watching the surveillance video?"

Max shrugged. "Not really, no."

"Can I volunteer?" she asked.

"Sure," said Boo. "If you want. It might be kinda boring."

"Boring is fine," said Andi settling in on the couch and angling the laptop so she could see it better.

The guys all went upstairs. Andi fixed her eyes on the surveillance video.

She tried to recapture that safe feeling she'd felt in the basement.

I came through the kitchen to look for everyone. The pretty girl was sitting on the sofa by herself. I went and sat down next to her. I liked her. She was quiet. More quiet than I was used to.

On the monitor, Andi could see the guys situate themselves in a circle next to the closet. She smiled, trying to imagine what they were saying to each other.

NIGHT VISIONS

The words "light as a feather, stiff as a board" kept popping into her head."

After a while, she saw them all get up and come back downstairs. When they came through, they announced they were splitting up and sending two guys back down to the basement. Alone. Sam and Boo.

Chaz and Max went back upstairs. Not long after that, she heard on the walkie-talkies that they were going to meet back in the living room.

Chaz came and sat down next to her. "I think we're going to call it. Not much is happening."

"Sometimes you just get a quiet night," said Max.

Boo sighed. "I hate when this happens."

Without another word, they all started packing up equipment. Andi helped peel tape off the electrical cords and pack everything up.

Within an hour, the house was back the way they'd found it and they were walking out the door. Boo was the last one out of the house.

NIGHT VISIONS

He turned the key in the lock. "Well that was a big, fat bust," he said.

As they were backing out of the driveway, Andi glanced back at the gargoyle that had greeted her on the way in. She imagined it was saying good-bye. Glad the night was over, she leaned back in her seat, sighed with relief and closed her eyes.

"Miss Tanya," I shouted. *"You're not going to believe it."*

She appeared, but barely. I wasn't sure if she would. I knew she hadn't rested long enough, and I was right. I could see right through her.

"What's all the racket?" said Tanya. *"What are you hootin' and hollerin' about?"* She was already fading again.

"Shadow Thing!" I hurried to explain. *"It's gone!"*

NIGHT VISIONS

She squinted her empty eyes at me. "*What do you mean it's gone? Where did it go?*"

"*It's just gone.*"

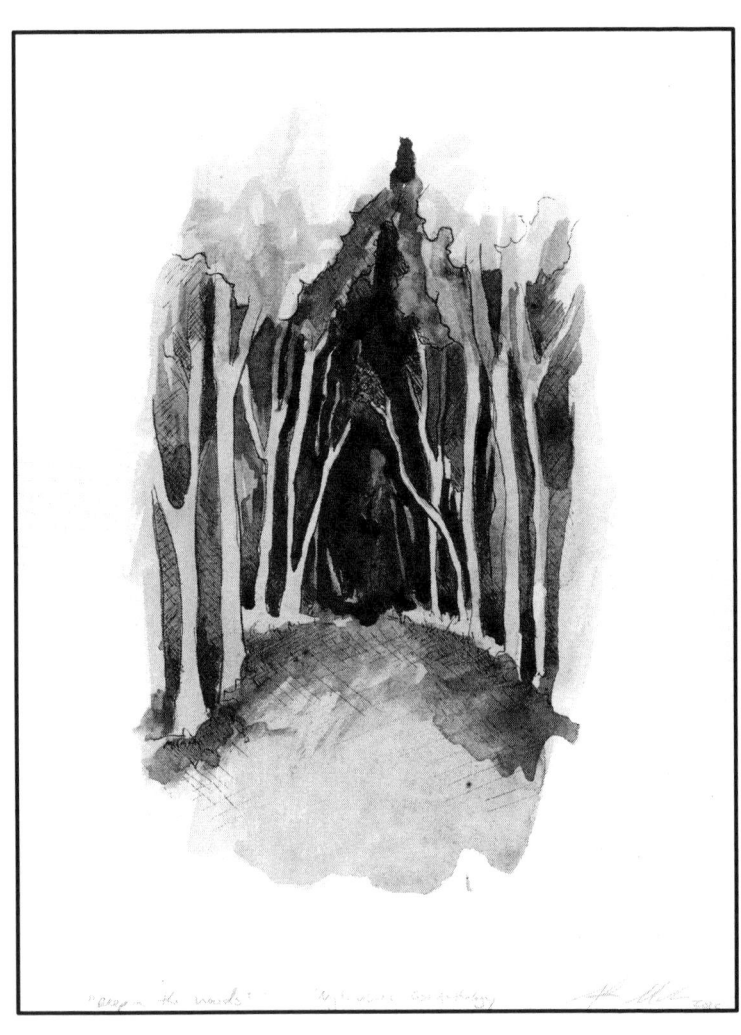

THE COTTAGE

By Crystal Brutlag
Retreat Participant – Contest Winner
Inspired by a Former County Poor Farm in Minnesota

The teens emerged from the woods and huddled in front of the dark, abandoned cottage, their eyes as round as the full moon overhead. The brilliant light illuminated the sagging stairs, with floorboards rotted away after many years of disrepair.

"Should we go inside?" Meg whispered, barely loud enough for anyone to hear over the chirp of the crickets.

"Let's wait for Serena to get here," Elisabeth whispered back. Her fingernails dug into Meg's arm.

Jenn leaned forward. "Mike told me that he and his friends ran screaming from the cottage when they came here."

Meg rolled her eyes at the mention of Jenn's boyfriend. Elisabeth loosened her grip on Meg's arm and glared back. Sometimes Jenn mentioned him just to upset Meg.

"I'm sure that's not true," said Elisabeth. "Why would they tell anyone that they were so scared they ran away screaming? I mean, really. A group of football players? Admitting they were afraid of a little ghost?"

Jenn scowled. "If it's just a little ghost, then why are you clinging to Meg's arm?"

Elisabeth released her grip on Meg. "We walked through the woods under a full moon. It's a little creepy. Who knows what's out here."

"Or who." Meg shuddered.

"Hey guys!" A perky voice pierced the air, in the same clearing they had emerged from. Serena grinned. "Jumpy much?"

Elisabeth's heart beat faster. "Perfect timing, Serena." The girls laughed, their chuckles airy and hesitant.

Serena looked at the stairs leading to the wraparound porch. "We'll have to be careful on the wood," she observed.

"Maybe we should just leave," Jenn suggested. "I mean, if Mike and his friends were scared . . ."

Meg and Elisabeth tensed again. Why did Jenn always feel the need to mention Mike? If she was upset that her friendship with all the girls wasn't what it once was, she had no one to blame but herself. She made her choice.

Jenn knew Meg had a crush on Mike since forever. Meg had even gone on a couple of dates with him. He seemed interested in her, until the night of the football captain's party, when Jenn's car broke down. Of all her options, Jenn called Mike to come rescue her. After that they were inseparable; Jenn and her knight in shining armor.

Serena bubbled with laughter. "Mike and his friends were scared? What a bunch of wusses!"

Jenn shifted her weight from one foot to the other. "No, they're not! What if there really is a ghost in there?"

"Then we talk to it." Serena pulled her phone out of her pocket, pulling up the notepad.

"We talk to it?" Jenn asked in disbelief.

"Yeah. Look, if you want to stay out here and wait, that's fine. But I've been ghost-hunting with my mom. So I'm going in. If there's a ghost here, I want to talk to her."

"To her?" Elisabeth chimed in.

Serena nodded. "I did some research on the house. The last owners were Edward and Esme Earle. Edward ran off with Esme's cousin, and she lived out the rest of her life alone in the house. She died when she was eighty-two."

"And she lived here alone until she died? That's impressive." Elisabeth looked back at the cottage with awe.

Serena nodded. "That's probably also why no one else wanted to buy the house after her. She may not have been able to take care of it properly by the end."

Jenn shuddered. "Who would want to live all the way out here by themselves? And her husband ran off with her cousin? What a jerk!"

Always in tune to her best friend's feelings, Elisabeth noticed Meg's jaw clench and positioned herself between them. "Yeah, he and her cousin deserved each other, didn't they?" Meg murmured.

"What did you say?" Jenn asked.

"Nothing."

Serena opened her bag. "Okay, let's go inside. You all have flashlights. I brought along some of my mom's ghost hunting tools."

Jenn burst out laughing. "Ghost hunting tools? Come on. I thought we were just going to walk into a dark, empty house and look around."

Serena couldn't help but feel annoyed. Why had they even invited Jenn along? "So, if it's just a dark, empty house, why did Mike and his friends run screaming from it?"

Jenn stepped back and looked at the ground.

"Anyway, as I was saying," continued Serena, "I didn't bring much, but I have an EMF meter, a thermometer, and a recorder."

Meg and Elisabeth stepped closer. Serena felt a flutter of excitement as she showed them the gadgets. Her mom always did this when they were accompanied by someone who was new to ghost-hunting. But now, on her first solo ghost hunt, she was the leader!

"What do they do?" Meg asked in a hushed tone.

"The EMF meter will give an electrical reading, and this one also shows the temperature, but I brought along a thermometer so that we can have two people looking at the temperature. The recorder picks up any audio that we might not actually hear." Serena shoved the gadgets back into her bag and turned on her flashlight. "Ready to go inside? First we need to put our phones in airplane mode, so they don't interfere with the EMF meter."

After a moment of hesitation the girls nodded, pulling their phones from their pockets. They began to follow Serena to the cottage's porch. The rough wood railing skimming their hands, as they gingerly worked their way up the rotting stairs. Doing a brisk tip toe across the porch, Serena reached the front door, and turned the doorknob, hoping the door would open. With a squeak of the hinges, the door swung open and Serena breathed a sigh of relief. Word around town was that a construction crew had started renovating the cabin and she had been worried the door would be locked.

As their flashlights blazed in the dark house, details of the grain of the wood on the floor and the walls came into view. The cottage seemingly came to life as the moonlight shined through the wall of windows by the backyard. The deteriorating, wooden furniture that once filled the cottage had been removed, but the smell of rot and mold lingered. "I guess it's true," Serena said. "Someone actually bought the cottage." Everyone in town had heard the rumors, but it was hard to imagine anyone wanting this old dump.

Glancing at the toolbox by the wall, Serena wondered what would happen to Esme after all the renovations were done. Would Esme be displaced from the home she had refused to leave, even after death? Serena made a mental note to ask her mom about that.

"So what do we do?" Jenn asks. "Sit in the middle of the room and hold a séance?"

"No, we never summon the ghost," Serena explained. "The top floor doesn't feel right to me. Let's go downstairs."

"Y-you want us to go downstairs?" Elisabeth stuttered.

"Yeah, I just feel like we'll have a better chance of talking to Esme if we're there. It's a gut instinct."

"A gut instinct?" Jenn rolled her eyes again, while Serena worked hard not to roll hers back in return. What was with the constant repetition? Jenn had bordered on intolerable before she started dating Mike; she was even worse now.

"Yes. My mom always tells me to trust my gut during investigations. Let's go downstairs."

Serena began her entrance into the basement, taking time to feel each step. The basement was dark, requiring the girls to move slowly down the stairs. The footsteps of her friends echoed behind Serena; three footfalls, a long pause, three footfalls. Serena hid her smile as her flashlight beam illuminated Meg and Elisabeth, still clutching each other's hands after the last step, with Jenn gripping the back of Elisabeth's shirt.

Once downstairs, Elisabeth shrugged Jenn off, taking a step away. "So what's next?" she whispered.

NIGHT VISIONS

A swath of moonlight shined through a single window in the cement wall of the basement. The window was too high to reach and too small to climb through, even if they could manage to get up to it.

Finding a spot on the unfinished floor, Serena sat down and removed the gadgets from her bag. Once they realized they were staying, the other three moved to the moonlit strip and sat cross-legged on the floor. Serena turned on the EMF meter, taking a reading of the basement. "There's no electrical reading to speak of."

"What does that mean?" Jenn asked.

"It means that when the meter starts to light up, a ghost is nearby. Hopefully."

"Hopefully?" Jenn croaked. "I'm starting to have second thoughts about this."

"Well, get over them, or get out. But you're leaving alone. Right, ladies?" Serena turned to Meg and Elisabeth, who, after a moment's hesitation, nodded.

"Right," Meg squeaked.

"I'll stay," Jenn said.

Serena clicked the record button on the audio recorder she'd brought along. "It's 62 degrees, right now. If the temperature dips lower, that could mean that Esme is in the room. This is Serena, and I am in the abandoned cottage off of Old Highway 10 with Meg, Elisabeth and Jenn. We are here to see if we can talk to the ghost that is said to reside here."

Serena looked up and grinned at her friends, turning off her flashlight and placing it on the floor in front of her. She asked then to do the same. They eyed her warily and turned off their flashlights.

"Hello!" Serena called out into the air. "My name is Serena, and I brought some friends with me today. Is anyone here?"

Meg, Elisabeth and Jenn held their breath. Nothing happened.

"We mean you no harm. We've heard there might be a spirit trapped in this cottage. If you're here, would you make this device light up? All you have to do is come closer to me."

Serena extended her arm to the side. "If you're behind me, I give you permission to touch me to let me know you're here."

Elisabeth took in a quick breath, leaning over to Meg. "Did she just tell the ghost that it can touch her?"

"Yep," Meg whispered back.

"I hope it doesn't touch me," Elisabeth whispered. "That would freak me out even more!"

Yet again, nothing happened.

"We'll just sit here for a little while, and if you decide you'd like to talk to us, you can come closer to this device and turn on my flashlight."

They listened to the silence, not taking their eyes off the light from the top of the EMF reader. Despite an hour of waiting, the EMF meter remained unchanged, and the flashlights stayed off. A sense of restlessness settled in, as the girls became wary of trespassing in an old, dilapidated building way past curfew.

Mom would be so mad at me if she knew, thought Serena.

Going for one last attempt, Serena spoke into the air "If you don't want to talk to us, we'll leave. But we wanted to come here tonight to let you acknowledge that you're here. We know you've been living within these walls alone. We also know that others have come here on a dare, to be scared. They haven't entered respectfully. We come in respect, to remember you."

Serena glanced down at the thermometer. Her breath caught in her throat, "The temperature is going down."

Going down was an understatement; the temperature was plummeting.

"Hi!" Serena's voice bubbled with enthusiasm, while the other girls sat stick-straight again. "You've joined us! Will you step closer and light up this device so we know for sure you're here?" The lights on the EMF meter began to light up from green to red.

The temperature in the basement continued to drop. "We're so happy to meet you! Can you turn on the flashlight if we ask you questions? Turn it on if the answer is yes, and leave it off if the answer is no." The flashlight turned on slowly. "Thank you! Would you please turn it off now?" The flashlight flickered off. "Thank you. I'd like to ask you some questions. Would that be okay?" The flashlight turned on and off.

"Did you live in this house?"

Elisabeth's flashlight flickered on. Elisabeth grabbed Meg's hand again as the flashlight flickered off.

"Did you live here with your husband?" Serena asked. The flashlight in front of Meg flickered on, before turning off again. "Can you tell us your name?"

An airy voice whispered in Meg's ear, "Esme."

Upon hearing the voice, Meg felt Esme's presence; not just the cool air that a ghost can bring, but the emotions that radiate from it.

"Is your name Esme? Esme Earle?" Serena asked.

Meg's gaze lingered in the direction of Serena. Why was she asking what Esme's name is when she'd just whispered it? Meg glanced at Elisabeth, whose attention was focused on Serena. A chill ran through Meg as she realized that she was the only one who'd heard the whisper.

The flashlight in front of Jenn turned on and off.

"Thank you for answering our questions, Esme. I did some research on your house before we came because I wanted to know who we'd be meeting. I read that your husband left you for your cousin. I can't even imagine anything so terrible! Is that true?"

The flashlight remained off, no response. Serena felt her heart sink; she was having so much fun getting to know a ghost on her own, without her mom for once. Now, she was afraid she'd shut down the interaction by asking such a personal question too soon. Serena searched for a way to bring the ghost back. When she saw the look on her friends' faces she thought they finally understood why she loved ghost-hunting so much, even if they were a little freaked out. She didn't want the experience to end after just a few flicks of the flashlight.

After Serena asked about Edward, Meg began to feel an ache in her chest as she remembered the day she saw Mike walking down the hall at school, holding Jenn's hand. It felt like a punch in the gut to see them together. It must have felt worse for Esme when she found out that her husband left their marriage for her cousin! Meg clenched a fist as she imagined the pain Esme must felt when she found herself all alone. Her outrage over Esme's loss mingled with the anger toward Jenn and Mike that simmered inside her.

Meg understood why Esme would flee at the reminder of something so painful; Meg wouldn't have stuck around either. Still it would have been nice to have more of an opportunity to talk to Esme, to let her know that she wasn't alone.

NIGHT VISIONS

The air in the room grew cold again.

"*Yyesss.*"

The hushed word echoed through the air, as Serena turned to face her friends, goose bumps prickled her arm. Meg was the first to pull herself out of her reverie after hearing the ghost's voice, glad this time she wasn't the only one to hear it.

Esme's anger felt tangible now, and Meg found comfort in it. In a sense, Esme understood how Meg felt, losing the guy she cared about to someone she trusted. The anger assaulted Meg as coldness washed over her body and her hand curled into a fist.

She began to think it would be a good idea to take a swing at Jenn. Meg glared at her, her hand stillcomfo balled at her side, her teeth clenched. She'd never thought about punching anyone before. Where had that impulse come from? The anger that welled up in her chest still burned inside her; an anger stronger than anything that she had ever felt. It was almost as if she had tapped into Esme's emotions, but that wasn't possible. Was it?

Serena glanced at Meg and saw her clenched fist as she glared at Jenn. She looked ready to pounce. "Meg, are you ok?" she asked.

"I'm really tired. And I'm a little weirded out by everything that has happened here tonight." Meg turned back to Serena, her fist unclenched as she notice Serena staring at it. "I'm sorry, but I think I need a little fresh air."

Serena sighed. "That's okay. Why don't you go outside and wait, while we finish up."

Meg stood, giving one last cold look at Jenn before nodding.

"Do you want me to come with you?" Elisabeth prepared to push herself off the floor.

"No, you stay here and finish this out." Meg turned and ran up the wooden steps. She glanced around the top floor of the empty moonlit house and shivered, before she exited through the front door and ran off the porch. She was happy to stand still for a minute, outside the cottage, and took a deep breath. She tipped her neck to one side, then to the other.

Unfortunately the silence was interrupted by the front door opening. Jenn had followed her outside.

"What are you doing out here?" Meg growled.

Jenn shot a quizzical look in Meg's direction. "I didn't want to be down there from the start, so when you left I took the opportunity to leave too."

Meg shook her head, wondering why Jenn sat through all of that, even though she didn't want to. "If you didn't want to be in there, why did you even come along tonight?"

"Because you guys invited me."

"We invited you because you interrupted us while we were talking about it. We thought you'd be with Mike tonight."

"Mike has to watch his little brother. He invited me to come hang out, but I thought that might be a little weird." Jenn locked eyes with Meg.

Meg was sure, without a doubt, that Jenn knew exactly how much talking about Mike bothered her.

"It would have been better than being here," Meg said. "He actually wanted to spend time with you."

Meg ignored the stab of pain that accompanied her words.

Jenn let out a sharp laugh. "What are you saying? I won the boy, so I'm not allowed in your little group anymore?"

Anger flashed through Meg. "You only wanted to be in our little group when it suited you, why should you care?" She began to feel the same surge of emotion that she felt in the basement before she'd felt the urge to punch Jenn. Meg had a sudden fear that Esme was with her, feeding her anger with her own; which startled her, but was equally comforting.

Meg stepped closer in the Jenn. "I should lock you in the basement and leave you there to rot," she said, under her breath.

Jenn stumbled back, confused. And afraid.

Again Meg's anger dissipated, and she was confused by her own words. Where had that come from?

Thankfully the door creaked open, as Serena and Elisabeth joined them outside.

"How are things out here?" Serena asked.

Elisabeth hurried to Meg's side. "Are you ok?" she whispered into Meg's ear.

"Just fine," Meg assured her friend. "We had a chance to talk," she added with a grin. Elisabeth smiled back, a bit of uncertainty in her eyes.

As the girls began to make their way back to town through the woods, Meg saw a wary look on Jenn's face. There was satisfaction knowing Jenn was unsettled by their conversation. The anger she seemed to draw from Esme's spirit did not leave her as they got further away from the house. It seemed to cling to her, like a wet t-shirt.

Meg had the strange sense that she did not leave the house alone. Although that thought should bother her, she found an odd comfort in it. She wondered what sort of revenge Esme would take on her cousin if she could.

I can find a way to get even with Jenn.

THE LIFT

By Sammy Sarzoza
Award Winning Screenwriter
Friend of Ghost Stories Ink
Inspired by David Oman's House, located 150 feet from 10050 Cielo Drive and El Coyote

Tyler woke from his peaceful slumber and rolled out of his cheap futon bed. He shuffled across the room to the panel windows and yanked open the blinds. The only benefit of his rundown Koreatown studio apartment in Los Angeles was the view. He wasn't sure how he got so lucky – the vista of the downtown skyline should have been way out of his price range.

NIGHT VISIONS

Normally, at about this time, he'd be basking in the morning sunrays – it was his favorite part of the day, but today was different. Puffy grey clouds covered the sky for as far as the eye could see. On top of that, a thick haze in the air rendered all the skyscrapers invisible in the distance. It was quite eerie, but it seemed fitting since it was Halloween. It's said that it never rains in Southern California, but the truth is it's not always sunny.

As Tyler walked to his bathroom, he had a sense that this day would be a little strange - it was akin to the same feeling he got just before an earthquake hit. In the bathroom mirror, he studied his face and ran his fingertips around the edges of his eyes and mouth searching for any signs of aging. To most, this would be considered gross vanity, but to him, it was a daily assessment of his value, like checking a stock quote. Tyler was an actor, and like everyone who makes their living on their looks, his main antagonist was time.

NIGHT VISIONS

After a good fifteen minutes of high-intensity inspection, he made a pot of coffee before his daily five-mile run. The jolt of caffeine helped get his feet going for the torturous training. The coffee was Folgers and not very pleasing to his particular palate. He much preferred the grounds found at one of L.A.'s best-known coffee shops, The Coffee Bean & Tea Leaf, but rent was expensive in L.A. For the time being, he was bound by a budget. As the coffee brewed he started getting ready, while he searched on his phone for the day's forecast. To Tyler, the only thing worse than running, was doing it in the rain. The weather app told him that the rain should stay at bay in the morning, but forecasted a downpour by nightfall. Being the Halloween forecast, the screen displayed a spattering of cartoon jack-o-lanterns.

Tyler hated this holiday more than any other, even as a child. He enjoyed the element of dress up, that was the actor in him, but there was just something about the day itself. He could never quite articulate it to anyone, he had always felt an evil in the air every October the thirty-first. He often pondered that maybe with so many people focused on the holiday's dark themes, the masses inadvertently summoned some sort of darkness from the depths of the earth. These thoughts continued to hop around in his head during his run as he navigated the uneven city sidewalks. Even though it was early, the many pedestrians he passed were already in the holiday spirit, donning costumes that ranged from silly to downright scary. All the pageantry reminded Tyler that he had yet to put any effort into his own costume for the night and would probably pay a hefty price for it.

    Tyler didn't even want to go to the party, but his friend David personally invited him. If he didn't go, he'd look bad skipping out after he'd already agreed to show up. Plus, he knew the place would be packed with some high-level industry types, the kind that could possibly make careers. David was a working actor, every actor's dream, on a long running series about cops and crimes. Tyler met him at the birthday party for a friend that was held at the historic Roosevelt Hotel on the west end of Hollywood Blvd. He and David hit it off right away. They were both from the Midwest and liked the same music and sports teams. Since their meeting, David had been generous with his time, providing Tyler with a lot of good advice concerning his career.

Tyler's career weighed heavily on his mind as he completed his run. He had a big audition in the afternoon; one he had been looking forward to for weeks. It wasn't "the" audition yet, but to get to "the" audition, you had to survive round after round of cold read auditions and the dreaded 'water meetings'. Tyler had learned to accept this part of the process. He figured no one loved every aspect of his or her job, so why should acting be any different? Plus if the rumors he heard from his agent were true, he was willing to put up with a bit of run around.

The word around town was that Tyler was shortlisted for a lead role by a very brilliant up-and-coming Polish director for his next movie. There were whispers in every office within the TMZ (Thirty Mile Zone) that the movie was about a detective trying to catch a serial killer ghost. On its face, the premise of the film sounded silly. But Tyler heard through the grapevine from the select few who read the super-secretive script that it was brilliant, and had everything Hollywood loved: blood, bullets, and sequel potential.

Back in his apartment, now drenched with sweat, Tyler began his recovery process of protein powders and vitamin mixtures; he recited the lines he learned for his audition. The casting people told him to prepare a scene from a detective movie, any era. The obvious choice was the classic film *Chinatown*. Normally, Tyler hated the obvious choice, but this time, according to his agent, it was the right choice.

Chinatown was L.A., and the only thing people in this town loved as much as their own image was their fair city. Tyler mechanically repeated the words over and over as he moved on to the rest of his morning routine. He said them in the shower, as he applied his organic facial creams, and in between bites of his mostly vegetable breakfast. He believed in over-preparation and was determined to leave everything on the table today. Shots like this didn't come around too often.

Fully dressed and put together, with every strand of his short hair in place, he gave himself one last look in a full body mirror that hung on his door. He grinned approvingly at the handsome, square-jawed face that reflected back at him. Before leaving, he grabbed a wad of cash that lay on a nearby table and stuffed it into his jeans pocket. The cash came from his job slinging margaritas and other feel-good drinks at El Coyote, a Mexican restaurant on Beverly and Fuller near the CBS lot.

It was a good job, and in his six months of being there, he served a host of Hollywood players. That's the thing about the iconic L.A. places; everyone has to go to them at least once, just to say they've been there. In fact, the job had led to him getting his agent, Calvin.

NIGHT VISIONS

Calvin had been in one night waiting for a date and recognized Tyler from a viral video he saw on YouTube. Later, after he signed with Calvin, Tyler laughed at the irony. Months of auditions, cold calls, meetings, and thousands of dollars spent on headshots, and he got signed off of a dumb video he did with a friend that took about 20 minutes to make.

Since acquiring Tyler into his stable of fellow young and hungry talent, Calvin had been hustling. Over the past few months, he was getting him bit roles in TV shows and a spattering of commercials. The work was starting to get constant now, and Calvin was pushing for him to quit his day job and commit full-time to acting. Tyler wanted that, but still liked the security of a consistent paycheck. Recently, Calvin put more pressure on him by asking if he'd seen any of the ghosts that reportedly haunted the restaurant. Tyler assured him that he had not seen anything every time he asked, in fact, he was convinced Calvin was making it up. That is, until the week prior.

NIGHT VISIONS

After the restaurant closed for the evening, Tyler had begun his cleanup duties. It was quiet, as it usually was, until he heard a woman's laugh from an adjacent room. He knew it couldn't be any co-workers because all the female staff had left long ago. Just as he stepped out from behind the bar to investigate the source of the noise, he froze as he watched a pregnant, blonde woman in a white dress walk across the dining room area and disappear into the air. Tyler wondered if it was the spirit of the actress who many claimed ate her last meal at the restaurant before she was killed in the Hollywood Hills. He could never remember her name, but saw her picture many times. This experience gave more weight to Calvin's argument, and Tyler hated that. Still, he promised himself if this audition went well, he'd tell Calvin he'd quit El Coyote, whether he got the role or not.

After a good hour and a half fighting his way through traffic in his late-model Honda Civic, Tyler had made his way to the Burbank office building about forty-five minutes early for his audition. He didn't want to leave anything to chance; he'd learned not to toy with the L.A. traffic gods and that it was always prudent to leave extra early for appointments. With some time to kill, he decided to take a stroll and admire the decadent storefronts of the kitschy shops. He always wondered who bought the stuff displayed in the windows, things like rhinestone-covered statues of elephants or jackets made of feathers. As he continued his trek down the sidewalk, he came across a vintage shop. An odd collection of non-battery powered toys, outdated electronics, and wildly printed shirts were showcased in a sort of beautiful chaos in the multiple panes of windows that faced the street. Tyler thought this would be a great chance to maybe find a costume for the evening's festivities on the cheap.

He walked into the shop and was smacked in the face with a repulsive, potent odor. The aroma was similar to used athletic gear that had been baking in a closed car in the summer sun. He wanted to escape, but it wasn't the worst smell he'd ever inhaled. For a short time, a few summers back, Tyler had dated a roller derby girl. He'd attend her practices in a small, stuffy, dank warehouse with limited ventilation. By the end of most practices, he'd be nearly gagging at the smell that had accumulated with a gaggle of girls skating and sweating for over ninety-minutes. So if he could handle that, he could handle this, especially if he could save a buck or two on a costume.

    The guy behind the counter seemed indifferent to Tyler's entrance. In his mid-sixties, the overweight man with a mop of unkempt salt and pepper hair, shoved a slice of pizza into his mouth while his eyes were locked on the pages of an old Hollywood news magazine. Tyler weaved his way around the piles of knick-knacks and tchotchkes until he came to a large area of used vintage clothes that spanned from the 50's to the 80's. He smiled at the variety of options, but not at the prices. The tags displayed prices that seemed a little steep, but it was still a little less then what he was expecting to spend on a costume, so he continued to peruse the racks for something that spoke to him. After a few minutes, he found a vibrantly colored shirt that just screamed, "Flower Power." He considered the prospect of dressing up as a hippie. He held up the shirt to his lean frame, and it looked like a perfect fit. He inspected the interior to see if he could locate a size. Inside, on the back of the collar had an interesting tag that read: 'Shirt is property of W. Frykowski.' Tyler wondered if that was even a name, and if so, from what country it hailed. Either way, he continued to scan the store in see if he could indeed piece together his intended costume, and after some searching, he did, from the bellbottom pants to a far-out leather headband.

Tyler failed at persuading the curmudgeonly shopkeeper to do him a solid and work with him on the total tab, but the time Tyler just saved not having to pick through overpriced and expensive mass produced costumes at some mall or department store was worth the few extra bucks. In addition, he thought he may be able to work at least the shirt into his normal wardrobe. A few ounces lighter from his loss of paper, Tyler hit the street and headed to his audition. In the cloud-covered sky, the sun was threating to burn its way onto the earth below. In this town, even El Sol was desperate to be seen, lest it too be forgotten like the dulled names of the old time entertainers whose stars lined the Hollywood streets.

Tyler walked out of the office building all smiles. He was sure he'd just nailed it. Everyone in the room had loved him and told him as much, a usual "no-no" in the biz. His reading was flawless, he felt as if he'd channeled Jack Nicholson himself. They told him to have Calvin call them to set up a meeting next week. They also said to expect pages from the real script.

Normally, Tyler wouldn't get so excited, but the people in the room were "the people" – the people who held the purse strings, the people who made the real decisions. He called Calvin before he reached his car and told him the good news. The conversation was brief as Calvin told him he had a hundred phone calls to make before the day was done, but before the conversation ended, he made sure to mention he was going to quit his day job.

Traffic wasn't so bad on the return route. Most of the rat-racers were on their way back into the valley. In fact, it took almost as long for Tyler to find a parking spot on the jam-packed Koreatown streets then it did to drive there. Once he was inside his building, he hit the community laundry room. The ensemble from the vintage shop still carried a hint of the shop's reprehensible funk. While they washed, he caught up on all the industry chatter on his phone. During the much longer dry cycle, he thought he'd walk up to a nearby wig store to see if he could cop a cheap long locked hairpiece to complete his transformation into a flower child. In L.A., wig stores seem as abundant as cafes and taco trucks.

NIGHT VISIONS

Tyler made it to the main artery in the neighborhood, Wilshire Boulevard. The sidewalks were busy with pedestrians. Even the foot traffic in this city was thick during rush hour. The costumed revelers had increased since the morning and included school-aged kids dressed as heroes from the pages of the picture books and silver screen. Tyler noticed the clouds were darkening to a deeper, more ominous shade of grey, and the light from the hidden sun was fading fast from behind the blanket of clouds. Tyler hoped the rain would hold out during the duration of his excursion.

He finally made it to the shop off Wilshire and Western. A bright L.E.D. signboard flashed the store's name in bold, green letters: WIGS 4 U. He pulled the door handle, but it was locked. Tyler pressed his face against the glass door and gazed inside. All the lights were on, and he could faintly hear the sound of some sort of soulful R&B music. Tyler took a step back and saw a paper sign taped on the door that read: "Sorry, had to step out. Be back in one hour. Thanks –Jay." In the reflection of the door, Tyler scowled as he played with his hair. His God given hair would have to do, as he didn't have the time or patience to either wait or make a return trip.

He got back to his apartment unit with his warm and fresh smelling clothes in hand and looked out the window. Darkness had fallen, and the city lights twinkled in the distance. He grabbed his phone and scrolled through his text log trying to find the address of the party. He had to dig deep past log after log of the many female admirers he had been in contact with over the past few weeks. Finally, he found it. The text from David read: "*Near 10050 Cielo Drive. Look for house with big orange pumpkins. Hollywood Hills. Benedict Canyon.*"

Tyler groaned. He hated when people weren't specific and was learning to get used to it, as "general specifics" was the culture of this place. He remembered that David had told him earlier that the party started at 9:00 p.m., but he knew that meant it didn't really start until about 11:00 p.m. or so. More than "general specifics" there was also a general relaxed nature to the start times of almost all recreational activities. He kept scrolling on his phone, toying with the idea of bringing a date with him to the party. However, he decided that since the party would be partly about networking, it was best to be free to meet as many people as possible.

Having some time to kill before he hit the road, he decided to eat a quick protein heavy meal and watch a movie. His uncle, who was a big movie-buff, had recently sent him one of his favorite horror movies in the mail in the spirit of the Halloween season. Since the time Tyler told his uncle that he wanted to be an actor at about age fifteen, his uncle had been on a mission to make sure Tyler had an extensive movie education. At this point, his uncle's crusade was almost a wash as Tyler rarely took the time to watch the films he sent him.

Tyler removed the DVD from the manila envelope. The title was *Rosemary's Baby*. Intrigued,

Tyler popped it into his large computer and plopped down to watch it. It started out slow, but once it got going, he found himself fully engrossed in the reeling tale of paranoia and insanity. The movie was about an actor making a deal with some nefarious neighbors that involved his unborn son. As a struggling actor himself, he could understand the character's plight, and at the film's conclusion, he was left with an eerie feeling. The kind that wrenches your stomach akin to the way most people feel after witnessing an act of violence.

Around 10:00 p.m., Tyler began to get into costume to an "Of Monsters and Men" playlist. After his extensive preparation, he modeled for himself in his full-length mirror. Everything fit like it was tailored. He looked like such a hippie; it was as if he had walked out of a time machine from Woodstock. Tyler looked out the window and couldn't find a trace of rain anywhere. He gathered his wallet, keys and phone and stuffed them into various pockets and headed out the door.

NIGHT VISIONS

In the car, Tyler jammed out to The Beatles to get into the mood of his "character." He knew most of the songs except for one called "*Helter Skelter*" which he found to be a weird, chaotic tune. As he rolled down Sunset Boulevard, he enjoyed rubbernecking at the bevy of scantily clad beauties in devious outfits as they paraded back and forth in front of the hippest clubs like The Whisky A-Go-Go and The Viper Room.

Soon, Tyler reached the base of the hills and began his climb into the winding labyrinth of twists and turns. The hills were like a dark maze; maybe it was designed that way intentionally. Another way for the elite who owned the stilted manors to keep the people from the flat lands out. As Tyler's car creeped higher into the canyon, the GPS on his phone cut out. He pulled over to troubleshoot the problem and noticed that his phone had lost all signal. Frustrated, he tossed his phone into the passenger seat. He looked up the road and noticed that both sides were packed with parked cars. It seemed parking was as tight here as everywhere else in L.A. Tyler thought even if he found the house, he'd probably have to hike a bit anyway, if he even managed to find a spot.

Tyler parked at the first sight of a spot, got out of his car, and slammed the door. Given the last reading on his phone, he knew he had to be close. He began walking up the street in search of Cielo Drive. In the distance, he could see parties in full-swing inside the mammoth mansions. He found the excursion a bit more ominous than he expected. The lack of streetlights and excess of nature that surrounded the road seemed to amplify the gloomy ambience. Occasionally, a few echoes of laughs and playful screams hit his ears, causing him to jump.

Tyler slowly realized his hike was turning out to be a mistake in judgment. At this point, he couldn't seem to get the thoughts of an animal attack out of his head. He remembered reading online about a hiker who was attacked and killed by a rabid coyote. The hiker had gotten lost somewhere in Griffith Park after sunset.

Some tourists on a horseback ride found him the next morning. From their statement, they were met face-to-face with an unrecognizable body. Once they got his body to the morgue, they were able to I.D. him as Clinton Jennings, a character actor who had just gotten a reoccurring role on a series about a cop who could solve murders by talking to his dead partner.

Tyler tried thinking about anything else, but his mind kept going back to the coyote story. He paused to dig in his pocket for his cell phone but froze when he realized he'd left it in the car. Even though he knew he probably wouldn't have service anyway, there was a comfort in having it that eased the sense of fear. He smacked himself in the head, to dish out a bit of penance for his stupidity. He turned around to double back toward his car.

As he began backtracking, a pair of headlights poked up from the horizon. It was the first car he had seen since he began his walk. Tyler waved at the car. He thought it was worth asking the driver if they knew the area and could help him find this Cielo Drive. Miraculously, the car slowed down. As it approached, he recognized it as a 60's era Dodge Dart.

Tyler had an extensive knowledge of old cars. His dad was a gear head and made him accompany him to seemingly endless car shows as a kid. After a while, he began to learn the various makes and models to combat the boredom. From the looks of the approaching car, it seemed to be in mint-condition. This didn't surprise him too much. Tyler had seen many older cars in Southern California look like new. Where Tyler was from, the salt from the snowplows turned even the finest machinery into rust buckets.

The car pulled up close to him and he made his way to the driver side. The driver rolled down the window to reveal himself. He was a pretty unassuming, young fellow, around twenty years old. He had a waspy look to him, with a tuft of reddish-brown hair parted to the side and thick "Buddy Holly-esque" glasses. Tyler squatted down to talk to him.

"Hey there, bro, I'm wondering if you could help me. I'm looking for a house... Well, actually, I guess I'm looking for a street first."

The man adjusted his glasses, smiled and replied, "I'm glad to help, stranger. What's the street?" Tyler felt better at the aid of this Good Samaritan. "It's Cielo Drive. Do you know it?"

"Know it? I sure do. I've got a friend who lives up there. I'm on my way up there to visit him now. Do you want a lift?"

Tyler couldn't believe his luck and replied, "That'd be killer, man."

"Well then, hop on in. I'm always willing to give a ride to a stranger in need," said the man.

Tyler made his way to the passenger side of the car and got in. From the car radio, a Beach Boys song played very low. Tyler wasn't sure which song, but was certain it was their unmistakable, melody-heavy sound. As the man started to drive, Tyler took note of his stellar costume. He wondered if the man had gone to a vintage store for his ensemble, like himself.

"What's your name, partner?" the man asked.

"Tyler."

"Tyler, eh? I can't say I've heard that name before."

Tyler grimaced. He didn't think his name was all that odd.

"My name's Steve. Do you know the people who live in the house on Cielo?"

"Not really, a friend invited me."

"I heard the people renting the house are in the pictures. One's an actress and her husband is a director. Do you know them?"

"I don't." Tyler said, salivating at the news. Maybe this party could open him up to a whole new world. "Do you know anyone there, yourself?" Tyler questioned.

"Me? No. I just have a buddy who lives in the guesthouse. I got a radio I think he may want to buy."

"A radio?"

"Yeah, I fixed it up myself. Clean as a whistle, in and out. Plus, I added a few extra features."

"Huh, I guess people collect everything, these days."

"In fact, I met him just like I met you, driving around down here. It's easy to get lost," Steve said.

"You're telling me. Plus I had like zero bars."

"What do you mean, zero bars?" Steve asked, his voice thick with confusion.

"Like, reception."

"Really? I never have that problem up here."

The car began to slow as it made its way up Cielo Drive. Tyler could begin to see a row of illuminated houses on one side of the street. Both sides of the street were packed with cars. Tyler wondered where Steve was going to park. True to David's word, one of the houses had a massive orange pumpkin on the front steps, the kind usually seen only in blue ribbon competitions at state fairs.

"I think that was is it. We just passed it."

"You sure about that? There's nothing here." Steve said as he stopped the car in front of a pair of massive gates at the end of the drive.

"Sure there is. Look--" His words were lost in the space between himself and Steve as Tyler's eyes widened from sheer terror. Steve's face was bloody, and it looked like his left cheek had been sliced into two.

Steve reached out at Tyler and struggled to speak, "He--lp... me."

Panicked, Tyler searched feverishly for the door handle, desperate to escape the gruesome transformation of this kind do-gooder. Tyler finally got a grasp of the door handle and yanked it open.

He got out of the car and bolted down the dark street toward his friend's house with the giant pumpkin, not looking back for even a second. When he reached the door, he began knocking furiously, trying to catch his breath. When there was no answer, he began pounding.

Finally, the door opened. A loud blast of some EDM music emitted from inside. David stood in the doorway to greet him.

"I thought I heard a knock." David said.

Tyler was hunched over, his usually tanned face as pale as chalk.

"Tyler, what's the matter? You look like you've just seen a ghost." Tyler embraced David and pushed him inside, slamming the door behind them.

Tyler began to relay his experience to David. He expected David to laugh him off, but was surprised to hear comfort in David's voice as he told him the gruesome history of the hallowed road. He told him a tragic tale of a Hollywood starlet and her famous friends who were senselessly slain by a group of mentally manipulated monsters on an August night in 1969. He went on to also tell Tyler about a young man who was killed in his car just inside of the gates. It quickly began to sink in for Tyler that the young man was the one who gave him a ride. Anxious to put the event behind him, he made his way to the open wet bar for a drink.

After a good hour or so, Tyler began to ease into a party mood. The further away he got from the encounter, the more he tried to explain it away in his mind. He thought he could have imagined the whole thing or maybe it was a sick practical joke. He was sure an area with such a macabre past would draw those who would find fun in terrorizing others with pranks related to the crime. It was strange, with each passing hour, the less and less real his possible supernatural encounter seemed.

Later, as the party began to wind down, Tyler had acquired compliments on his costume and the business cards of several good industry contacts. That's not all he got; a cute girl dressed up as Sailor Moon offered him a ride down to where he parked his car. She had caught a bit of his story when he first arrived and was sympathetic to his paranormal plight. As they left, David checked with Tyler one last time to make sure he was okay. Tyler assured him that he was and told him that he just got a little spooked by the darkness that surrounded the area.

When Tyler and the girl got to his car, he made sure to get her number, as they planned to see each other later in the week.

"I know you weren't lying to David," she told him as she settled into her driver's seat. "I'm a sensitive, and the unrest in this area has made my head spin all night."

Before he could respond, she shut her door and drove away with a smile and a small wave.

By the time Tyler made it back to his apartment, it was 3 a.m., the time he'd heard others call "the witching hour." The building was like a silent tomb as he slogged up the steps. The sound of a cat scratching at his neighbor's door made him jump as he looked over his shoulder, the image of the young man in the car still strongly embedded in his mind.

As he entered his unit, he quickly locked the door behind him. His window blinds were still open. In the distance, the light from the downtown skyline glimmered. Tyler gazed out at the view and reflected on the entrancing sparkle of the city. He was struck by the thought that behind the beauty of the city was a glut of tragedy and horror.

"The prettiest places often hide the ugliest things," he said quietly to himself. He was completely unaware that he actually spoke the words in French, a language he had never spoken before.

A bolt of lightning shot down from the sky, followed by a boom of thunder. Tyler's reflection flashed in front of him. Despite his chiseled features and each strand of his short hair, perfectly in place, he looked tired. Without warning, a downpour began that was so thick, it clouded the view of the downtown towers. Tyler reached out to pull the blinds closed.

As the shades began to shut over his reflection, he thought he saw something different about himself. He wore the same hippy clothes, but for a moment his hair looked longer – shaggy almost. His jawline and the firm features of his face softened. The face looking back at him, was not his own. Tyler's brow furrowed in confusion as he pulled the shades back up. Then another flash of lightening brightened the sky, and the unfamiliar face was gone.

Tyler rubbed his eyes and took another glance at his reflection. Certain his eyes were playing tricks on him, he quickly closed the blinds. It had been a long, strange night. He had never been a fan of Halloween, but he was especially glad this one was over.

6 UNFORGOTTEN

Written by L. W. Edwards
Retreat Participant – Contest Winner
Inspired by a Poor Farm in Minnesota

Aaron thought he felt his line give a tug. He tried to not let himself get too excited. But he couldn't stop the spark of a thought. If he could just catch a fish, even better a big one, then they'd have to notice him. He flung his line up the shore and looked at the hook. His victory was short lived. Once again, there was nothing. Frustrated, he sat down on a nearby rotting log. The bark creaked under him as he propped his elbows on his knees and settled his chin into the palms of his hands.

"Did you hear that? It sounded like a twig broke." A man's voice broke through the nocturnal chirps of the lakeside night life.

"It was probably just one of us, stepping on a branch," said another man.

Aaron looked up from his perch on the log. He'd seen groups of people walking around the lake before. He'd even tried to talk to them, but they never seemed to hear him.

The two men moved closer to the lake's edge, looking out over the water. A woman followed behind them, but stopped behind the log where Aaron sat.

"This is where they say the boy drowned," one of the men said matter-of-factly. He pulled a small machine from his pocket. The light held steady at green. "They never did find his body. I'm going to use this K2 to sweep for electromagnetic energy in the area," he said to the other man.

NIGHT VISIONS

Aaron watched the younger man pick up a stick and toss it in the lake, breaking the glassy surface with ripples.

"He's here," the woman said, her voice tight with emotion.

Aaron turned his attention away from the men toward the woman.

"I see you," she said.

"What? Where? What do you see?" asked the bearded men, walking toward her.

The lady pointed her figure toward the log, "Right there," she said. "I see a young boy on that log."

Startled, Aaron pulled back, slipping off the log and landing on the ground with a dull thud.

"What was that?" that man asked, his eyes wide.

"We scared him," the woman said. "We don't mean to frighten you. We just want to speak with you. What's your name?" Her voice was gentle, it reminded Aaron of a woman who had spoken to him many years ago.

He was afraid to answer. He doubted she would even hear him, but she seemed to somehow be looking right at him. He cleared his throat and stammered, *"My name is Aaron."*

"I think I heard him say Aaron," the woman said, looking over her shoulder toward the men. "Is your name, Aaron?"

"Yes!" Aaron shouted, surprised by his own excitement.

The bearded man moved forward sweeping the K-2 around the log. Its lights flashed from green to red. "There's some sort of electromagnetic energy here," he mumbled, still moving the device from one side of the log to another.

Aaron took another step back, startled.

"I feel like you're scaring him," said the woman. "Let's put away the gadgets for a minute and just see if we can make him comfortable with us."

The man put the machine in his pocket, still watching the log. The woman stepped forward. She looked past the log, to the exact place where Aaron stood. She seemed to be looking at Aaron – possibly seeing him. The way she smiled made Aaron relax a little.

The man who had thrown the stick moved closer and stood beside the woman. "My great-grandfather was an inmate here when the little boy drowned," he said.

"Really?" the woman asked, glancing at the man quickly before returning her attention to Aaron.

"He was here," he said, looking down at his feet, "right here when it happened."

Aaron's eyes grew wide as he whispered, *"Sam?"*

"Was his name Sam?" the woman asked the man, her eyes still locked on Aaron.

"It was," the man replied. "How did you . . ."

"Aaron told me."

"I remember," Aaron trailed off, closing his eyes as if to block out the memory that wouldn't stay away.

Aaron's heart thumped in his chest. He knew he could get in a lot of trouble for sneaking out of the house without permission from Cook. He didn't care, he needed a minute to think. And he figured, if he managed to bring home a nice string of fish for dinner, all would be forgiven.

His fingers fumbled to get the squirmy worm on the hook. Frustrated, he tossed the pole aside and forced himself to take a deep breath. Maybe everything would be ok. Maybe that lady would want to adopt him and he'd finally have a real family, a real home. Maybe he'd finally catch some fish today.

He picked up his pole, found a big worm and plunged the hook through the middle of it. He'd only just tossed it out into the water when he heard footsteps behind him.

"Hey Aaron, what're you doing down here? You know Cook's looking for you," said Sam, wading through tall grass to get to him. "If you were a bright boy, which you ain't, you'd get back up to the house and sweet talk her." Sam glanced back toward the trail leading down to the lake.

"I'm fishing and thinking Sam. Leave me be," Aaron answered.

"The only thing you need to think about," Sam said, "is how you can stay on Cook's good side. If you don't, she'll surely lock you in the basement or maybe worse. She might do what she did to Tommy and tie your hands and hang them over the hook on the wall. Besides, what's so important, anyway?" Sam asked.

"If I tell you, will you go away and let me think?" Aaron shot back. He sat down on the rotted old log to watch his line.

"Yeah sure, just trying to help. What's a seven-year-old boy need to think so hard about anyways? All I think about is where my next meal is coming from," Sam said, sitting down on the log next to Aaron.

"Who says I ain't thinking about that," said Aaron. "You act like you were seven a hundred years old. God in heaven, Sam, you're only twelve," Aaron reminded him.

"Yeah, well what's on that pea-sized mind of yours?" Sam asked, reaching over to give the younger boy's shoulder a shove.

Aaron stared out at the lake. "I was in the kitchen this morning when that nice lady came through again to buy butter." He turned to Sam with a grin. "She smiled so sweet at me."

"Yeah, what of it?" Sam asked.

"She asked me my name, Sam. No one does that. You know they stick us here and forget about us," said Aaron.

Sam studied Aaron. "Are you thinking she might adopt you? You can just forget that. If a lady were to adopt any boy around here, it'd be me. I'm stronger and much better looking than you, and I know how to conduct myself. I came from money," Sam said, thumping his chest with his fist.

Aaron was quiet. He gave a tug at his pole, and to his surprise, it tugged back. Excited, he stood up and gave a big yank to fling the line up to the shore. Unfortunately, it was a big clump of wet, slimy weeds. He pulled them off of his hook. The big worm was gone. Who was he kidding? He was never going to catch any fish in this stinky old lake.

"Yeah, who could ever forget that you had parents?" asked Aaron turning back to Sam. "You talk about it all the time." He kicked at the ground. "Your dad used to be a big time railroad man, but now he's just dead, and your mom . . .she went and killed herself." The words came out before he could stop them. He watched Sam's face change from hurt to rage. Sam leapt from the log onto Aaron's back. Both boys rolled around and were tangled up like a sailor's knot when they heard Cook's voice. Fighting was forgotten instantly as they untangled themselves and dove for cover in the brush.

From their hiding place, they watched as Cook looked up and down the bank calling their names.

Knowing how mad she got, they didn't breathe until she was walking back up the trail to the big house.

"Man, look what you did! You went and got me in trouble." Sam gave Aaron a shove.

"You came looking for me. You always come looking for me," Aaron shot back, even though he felt sorrier than he'd ever felt, for saying what he did about Sam's parents.

"Have it your way. Stay if you want, but I'm going back to take my lumps," said Sam standing up. "You can't say what you did about my mom. My parents may be dead, but at least I know who they are. You don't have anyone, and you never did," said Sam. He brushed off his pants and headed up the trail.

Aaron called after him. "Sam, I'm sorry! I didn't mean it," Aaron called out to Sam. "I've just got to try to find that lady. You're right. I *don't* have anyone, but I need someone, too."

Sam stopped. He looked back at his friend, the little brother he never had. "That lady is gone. And you

NIGHT VISIONS

know there's no way off this farm till you get old enough. There's always someone watching the road, and you'd get lost in the woods."

"There's one way," Aaron said, pointing at the lake. "I think she lives on a farm on the other side of the lake."

"Aaron, that's crazy. You can't swim that far," Sam shouted.

Aaron ran toward the water.

"Come on, we can talk Cook out of her punishment," Sam pleaded. He ran back down the hill toward Aaron.

Aaron dove in and swam toward the middle. Sam kicked off his shoes and jumped in after him. He saw the top of Aaron's head go down.

It popped back up. Relieved, Sam pushed himself to go faster, but he was too far behind when Aaron went down the second time.

Aaron didn't come up again.

"My great-grandfather had been lucky," the man said, his voice breaking through the silence that had settled on their small group. "Another inmate was passing by, and they were able to help him back to shore. They looked for Aaron for a time, that is, as much time as you would look for a boy nobody wanted." The man paused, kicking at the dirt. "My great-grandfather never came to this lake again."

His voice was kind, and Aaron moved closer to listen. The woman followed. The bearded man pulled the gadget from his pocket and pressed a button to turn it on. A series of lights lit from green to red, then settle back to green. He raised the instrument up to the area beside the woman, and the lights lit up to red. His eyes grew large. Aaron ignored the man's machine and focused on Sam's great-grandson as he spoke.

"He finally got out of here," the man said. "But he couldn't save his best friend, and that always haunted him."

The group stood on the shoreline, looking across the lake toward the farmland Aaron had hoped to escape to.

"I've been having dreams ever since my great-grandfather died. I think my great-grandfather wanted me to come back here. He wanted me to tell about how Aaron was like his little brother, and he missed him when he was gone. That's why I came. To tell someone."

Aaron's body began to tremble. He hadn't been alone when he was living at the poor farm. Sam had been his family – his brother. And after Aaron's death, Sam had never forgotten him. Not in his whole long life.

Aaron heard a familiar voice say, *"I came back here after I died, trying to make you see. But you couldn't see me."*

NIGHT VISIONS

Aaron whirled around. He could see Sam, standing beside his great-grandson in his torn poor farm clothes, as if he'd never left.

"*Every time. You just kept jumping in. Again and again and again. I could never make you see me,*" said Sam.

"*I don't want to jump in anymore,*" said Aaron.

"*Then let's go,*" Sam said. "*Come with me to the other side of the lake. The fish are the biggest you ever saw, and your stomach never growls.*"

Aaron turned to smile at the lady before running to his friend.

Both boys, arms around each other's shoulders, walked up the trail together until they faded into the mist.

The lights on the man's instrument dropped from red to green. He waved the K-2 around, trying to make the lights spike to red again, but nothing happened.

The woman smiled. "The boy is at peace. His spirit has finally crossed over."

THE IN-BETWEEN

By Shawn McCann
Investigator – Ghost Stories Ink
Inspired by The Palmer House Hotel

PART I

The machine keeping him alive sounded out its duty, one beep at a time. Cindy watched the monitor report vital information, like blood pressure and heart rate. But the doctors said it was just a matter of time, these things would all stop working soon. Any day now.

The doctors had described it with fancy words that Cindy didn't really need to know. All she really understood was that he was in between. He probably wouldn't regain consciousness. But he was still hanging on. She wondered what that was like, to be in between life and death.

In any event, it didn't matter how long it would take. She was happy to be here for him now, as long as necessary. She was glad she'd made the trip to Alexandria. Even if the only hotel room she'd been able to find was in the next town over.

Cindy's mind drifted back to childhood memories. He'd been a typical mean, big brother. But after their father was killed in a car accident, their mother had been left to raise all five of them. Sanity was scarce. As the two youngest, Cindy and Roger were left to themselves. The three older kids wanted nothing to do with them, but the two of them had managed just fine.

She kissed her brother on the cheek before she left. "I'll be back tomorrow," she promised.

The drive to her hotel felt like a long one. All she had to do was get inside, get upstairs to her room, and crawl into bed. She had to be mentally ready for the inevitable, and only a full night of sleep could help with that. She glanced at the clock. 11:30. A full night's sleep was already out; she'd have to settle for a half-night.

She soon reached the sparsely used parking lot. It seemed that she was the only guest at the old hotel. The turn-of-the-century place was quaint, but she would have preferred to see a friendly face or two. Even if the sentiment was dictated by a chain hotel as a company standard, and inspired by a paycheck. She wished again that the hotel off the highway near the hospital would've had a vacancy. The man who'd checked her in had been nice enough, but he'd been the only other living soul she'd seen since she'd arrived.

Cindy fished her key from her purse and climbed the stairs to her room. Upon reaching door number eight, she stopped and stared. A red, rubber ball, like the kind her kids played with, sat perfectly positioned in front of her door. Too tired to think about it, she kicked it down the hall and it bounced once, twice, and then rolled to a stop. Satisfied, she slipped the key into the lock and gave it a turn.

She flipped on the light and walked in, tossing her purse on the bed and going to her suitcase in the corner.

BANG

A noise echoed from behind her. She turned.

It sounded like it had come from the bathroom. An uneasy feeling settled in the pit of her stomach.

"Hello?" she called out. She held her breath as she waited for a response.

Silence.

She returned her attention to her suitcase. She just wanted to slip into her pajamas and melt into bed.

CREAK

Another sound, more subtle then the last, came again from the bathroom. A bead of sweat ran down her back. She eyed her purse on the bed and considered running from the room.

"Is anyone there?" she asked, a slight quiver in her voice. After a long silence, she relaxed a bit. "I'm just tired and jumpy," she told herself, taking a deep breath. "And this place is old. Old buildings creak and settle all the time."

She walked hesitantly to the threshold of the bathroom and slowly peered inside. She had just enough time to let out a blood-curdling scream before two giant arms wrapped the disassembled shower curtain around her body.

Panicked, Cindy kicked and thrashed. But it was no use. The more she moved, the more she could feel the air running out. Her world went black.

When she awoke, she found that her hands had been tied to a metal pipe behind her back. She could feel the loss of blood to her hands as they started to tingle. The less she moved around the better it was, but the feeling of helplessness surged, making her act out in little fits of frustrated despair. No matter how hard she tried to call for help, her breathless attempt to scream came out as a whimper. It was as if her brain and her mouth had been disconnected. Her eyes squinted through the darkness, trying to see. There was nothing but blackness.

"Help," she managed to squeak.

Silence was the only answer.

As Cindy sat in the dark, overwhelmed by the quiet, she began to think about her family. Thoughts of her husband, her kids, and her dying brother rushed through her mind. Regardless of how competitive they'd been growing up, this was one race she didn't want to win.

A grumble and a clank startled her out of her thoughts. The noise was followed by a steady hum. Maybe it was a furnace kicking on? Cindy realized she must be in a basement. Maybe of the hotel? She squinted through the darkness, her eyes finally adjusting.

NIGHT VISIONS

She gasped as she noticed two round eyes staring back at her. As the form came into view she saw its grin, and the three round balls that made its body. A snowman. How random. If this was a basement, maybe it was a winter decoration in storage. She didn't like it looking at her. It seemed to be mocking her.

Thump. Thump.

Cindy twisted her head, trying to see where the new noise was coming from.

Thump. Thump.

Her mind raced to think of what it could be.

Thump. Thump.

It almost sounded like . . .a ball bouncing. She remembered the ball from the hallway. She swallowed hard, but the fear, the feeling of dread, grew with each bounce.

Thump. Thump.

And then, she heard it. A deep laugh. It was evil.

Her kids played with balls. They weren't supposed to be scary.

Her eyes darted again to the snowman as if he were the culprit. Maybe it was her imagination.

Thump. Thump.

And then the deep, heavy laugh came again.

The new pattern was set. Each time a new set of "thumps" arrived, the evil laugh followed. This was someone's idea of a sick game. She was somehow living in a horror movie.

Thump. Thump.

"Shut up!" Cindy screamed, surprised to hear her own voice, coming back into play.

"Whatever you are here to do, just do it," she said.

With her words, the noise completely stopped. No movement, no shuffling of feet. Nothing. Just dead silence. The furnace had even turned off.

The silence was comforting at first. Cindy didn't have to listen to the tortuous thumping. But, a new fear washed over her. With the bouncing, she at least knew that the person doing the bouncing was not near her.

But silence, now they could be anywhere. Sweat trickled off her forehead.

A hand reached through the darkness and touched her.

The blood-curdling scream that escaped from her lips was her last.

Part II

A scream ripped through the air.

"Richard," said Louise, sitting up in bed. "Did you hear that?"

"What the hell was it?" Richard asked.

Another scream erupted from down the hall. And then another. Louise and Richard ran from their room and into the hallway. There were only eight rooms on each floor; that left only seven to check.

They hurried down the hall and tried to figure out where the sound was coming from. But it was almost midnight. Most people had already gone to bed.

It was too calm and quiet for the horrific shriek they'd just heard.

The scream came again. This time they could tell it was from the end of the hallway on the left. They ran to the door. Richard knocked, and when no one answered, he jiggled the doorknob. It was locked.

"Are you ok?" asked Louise. "Is anyone in there?"

"Go get help," said Richard. "The front desk."

Louise rushed back down the hallway to the stairs.

"Hurry," said Richard.

Jeremy tried not to glance at his watch. He knew it would only be a few minutes later than the last time he looked. This new job was easy, but covering the night shift at the old hotel was a lot more boring than he'd thought it would be.

NIGHT VISIONS

He heard footsteps above, they reached the steps and hurried down, he strained his neck to see who was in such a hurry this time of night.

"Call for help," gasped the woman. She was standing in her nightgown. Her cheeks were flushed, and she looked upset.

"What happened?" asked Jeremy, picking up the phone.

"A woman," said the lady, trying to catch her breath. "We heard screams. Room eight."

Jeremy put the phone back down. The manager had told him about room eight. But it was only his third day, he hadn't had to deal with this yet.

"What are you doing? Call the police!" the woman demanded.

"I don't think . . ." said Jeremy.

"Fine, then I'll call them." She leaned across the desk and grabbed at the phone.

Jeremy stood up from his chair and paced behind the desk. "I don't really think we need to do that," he said. But she was already dialing.

"What do you mean," she hissed at him. "A woman was screaming, it sounded horrible."

"I know, but . . ."

"Hello, my name is Louise Hartfield. I'm staying at the inn. I would like to report an incident. We heard horrible screams, and I think something has happened." Her voice dropped to a dramatic whisper. "I believe someone might have been murdered."

Jeremy ran his hand through his hair. He couldn't grab the phone away from a guest. Now that the 911 dispatcher had heard the word "murder," they would probably have to send someone.

He heard more footsteps on the stairs. This time a man was rushing down them. He was wearing plaid pajama pants and a white t-shirt. "I heard it again," he said. "She screamed again. Are the police coming?"

NIGHT VISIONS

Jeremy swallowed hard. He hoped the rest of the guests would sleep through the commotion. That's just what he needed, everyone in the hotel all in a panic.

The lady covered the mouthpiece with her hand. "I had to call them myself," she hissed at the man, who Jeremy assumed must be her husband. "He wouldn't do it." She glared at Jeremy.

"It's not that I wouldn't," said Jeremy. "I was just trying to explain . . ."

"Well tell them to hurry," said the man. "You," he said to Jeremy. "Who is staying in room eight? Do you have a key?"

Finally having a job to do, Jeremy flipped through the book. He already knew no one was in room eight. The hotel wasn't full, and he knew they only used room eight if they absolutely had to. But it was best to double-check. Every now and then, someone actually requested it.

"No one is staying in room eight," he told the couple.

"The police are on their way," said the woman hanging up the phone.

Jeremy sighed and grabbed the set of master keys.

The man reached out for the keys, but Jeremy shook his head.

"I'm sorry, sir," said Jeremy. "I'm not supposed to give these keys to anyone. But since no one is staying in there, we can go check it out and you can see for yourselves."

The woman hesitated. "I don't want to see anything for myself. I think we should wait for the police."

"Louise," said her husband. "If someone was hurt, we should help them. We might be running out of time."

"But what if it's not safe?"

With the keys in his hand, Jeremy started up the stairs. "Let's go check it out," he suggested again.

The man and woman stopped arguing and looked at him.

Jeremy pulled his phone from his pocket. "I have my phone, we can call the police again if we need to."

The man nodded and hurried past Jeremy to lead the way. The woman followed behind, keeping her distance.

"It's here, down this way," said the man.

Jeremy nodded. He already knew that.

The man stopped before he got to the door. "What's that doing there?" He pointed to the red rubber ball. It was sitting in front of the door to room eight. "I didn't see that before?" He strained his neck to look around Jeremy to his wife. "Did you see that here before, Louise?"

Louise wrapped her arms around herself and shivered. "No," she whispered. "That wasn't here before."

Jeremy stepped around the man. "Excuse me, sir."

The man let Jeremy go by and went to his wife, wrapping his arm around her.

With his toe, Jeremy gently moved the red ball to the side. He fumbled through the unknown keys and cursed himself for not thinking to just grab the room key from the box, since no one was even staying here. He finally came to the key labeled "Master." He took a deep breath and inserted it into the keyhole. He pushed the door open, and a rush of cold air enveloped the three of them.

Jeremy was glad when Mr. Hartfield pushed past him to be the first inside. Jeremy flipped on the light and Mr. Hartfield stopped in his tracks. There was nothing wrong with the room. The bed was neatly made. The remotes were placed in an orderly fashion on the end table. There certainly wasn't a woman screaming or being murdered. Mr. and Mrs. Hartfield stared at each other, surprise evident on their faces.

"Maybe we are in the wrong room," said Mrs. Hartfield.

"Maybe we should knock on all the other doors and make sure everyone is ok," said Mr. Hartfield.

"No," said Jeremy quickly. The last thing he wanted was for them to wake everyone else up. "Maybe we should go back down and wait for the police," he suggested.

"Good idea," said Mrs. Hartfield, leading the way out of the room.

Jeremy sighed with relief and followed them out, locking the door behind them.

When the police officers arrived, the Hartfield's gave their statement while Jeremy tried to make himself look busy at the front desk.

"Please, you have to go check it out for yourselves," begged Mrs. Hartfield. "Go knock on the doors, make sure everyone is ok."

The officers looked at each other and sighed. Jeremy took the key from the box for room eight, and offered it to the officers.

"You must be new here, huh kid?" asked one of them.

Jeremy could feel his cheeks get warm and he knew he was blushing. "She pulled the phone away from me before I could explain."

"It's a slow night anyway," said the cop with a wink. "Besides, I get the impression explaining things to her might make this woman even more upset."

"Thanks for coming," said Jeremy.

"We'll just go take a quick peek at room eight," the other officer said to the Hartfields.

Mrs. Hartfield whispered to her husband in a voice that seemed loud enough that she intended for Jeremy to hear, "They sure aren't taking any of this very seriously."

Mr. Hartfield just shrugged.

The officers came back after a few minutes, "I think you're safe."

"There's definitely nothing out of place up there," said the other handing the room key back to Jeremy.

"Maybe someone was just having a bad dream?" suggested the first officer.

"Maybe," said Mr. Hartfield.

"If you're sure everything is alright," said Mrs. Hartfield.

"We are," said the officers together.

Mr. and Mrs. Hartfield headed back upstairs together, each glancing back over their shoulder at the officers and Jeremy more than once.

When they were out of sight, Jeremy said, "Thanks again for coming out, officers."

"No problem," said one.

As they left, Jeremy looked at his watch. An hour had gone by. "Well at least that killed off some time," he mumbled to himself.

Richard opened the door to their room and let Louise enter first. "I just don't get it," said Louise softly. "I know I wasn't just hearing things!"

"I know," said Richard. "I don't know what to think."

It was awhile before either of them were finally able to sink into sleep.

The next morning, Richard and Louise went about gathering their things and packing their bags. Neither of them mentioned the events from the previous night. Finally ready to leave, Louise made one last check under the bed and took a peek in the bathroom. Satisfied, she nodded at her husband. He held the door and took her suitcase for her.

They walked together down the hall and stopped. The red rubber ball was now in the middle of the hallway, near the top of the steps. Neither of them said anything, instead they hurried past it and down the stairs.

At the front desk, they saw the woman who had checked them in the day before. Her nametag read, "Shelly" and stated she was an "Assistant Manager."

Richard put their room key on the desk and sat down in the chair. Louise sat next to him.

Shelly picked it up with a smile. "Jeremy mentioned you had an eventful night."

Louise pinched her lips together. "I don't want to get anyone into trouble."

Richard's eyes darted toward Louise, and he patted her knee before she could say anymore. "You could say that," said Richard. "We're still not really sure what happened."

"There was a woman screaming," said Louise. "But no one seemed all that concerned about it."

Shelly just nodded. With a smile, she reached behind her for a binder on the shelf. She set it on the desk in front of her. The words, "Ghost Experiences" were handwritten across the front in black marker.

Richard and Louise looked at each other.

"Last night was a ghost?" asked Louise.

"I don't believe in that sort of thing," grumbled Richard.

"Well," said Shelly, "it was room eight, right?"

"Yes," said Louise.

"And you saw the red ball, right?" asked Shelly. "Jeremy said the ball was in front of the door."

Richard and Louise looked at each other again. "That's right," said Louise.

"Well, we don't talk about it much, but about thirty years ago, there was a murder here."

"Thirty years ago?" asked Louise, the confusion evident in her voice.

Shelly nodded. "This place was empty for a few months while the new owners took over and planned out some renovations."

"The same owners as now?" asked Richard.

"No, no," said Shelly. "The ones before the current owners now."

Richard nodded.

Louise leaned forward in her seat. "Get to the murder part," she said.

"It happened when the hotel was empty," said Shelly. "Apparently, the victim, Cindy, was in town to visit her dying brother at the hospital in Alexandria. I imagine her mind was preoccupied with that when she came looking for a room."

"And then what?" asked Louise. "What happened?"

"They think someone pretended the hotel was open and tricked her into staying here. It was horrific. The best that they can tell, is the attack began in room eight. They found the shower curtain from that room down in the basement. So they think it was used that to drag her down there."

Louise gasped.

"That's terrible," said Richard.

"Do you really think she's haunting this place?" whispered Louise.

"Well," said Shelly. "The red ball moves around. When it ends up in front of room eight, it's usually accompanied by some sort of paranormal activity or ghostly encounter."

"What do you mean by paranormal activity?" whispered Louise.

Shelly gave a shrug. "Sometimes people hear screams. Sometimes, they hear a thumping noise down the steps. Other times people report feeling cold spots, stuff like that. But usually, the ball is involved somehow."

Louise nodded.

"Humpf," grunted Richard. "I've never believed in that sort of thing before, but I know what I heard last night. And it was definitely a woman screaming."

"It's not an easy thing to wrap your head around," said Shelly with a smile. "Personally, I think Cindy just wants us to remember her and not forget about her."

Louise nodded.

"Well," said Louise. "If all that is true, then I hope someday, she finds her peace and leaves that horrific moment to the ashes of time."

Richard and Louise stood. Louise shivered a little as a chill passed by them and seemed to accompany them to the front door. But to Louise, it felt more comforting than terrifying. Maybe this was Cindy's way of thanking them for hearing her?

Louise left, wondering about the in-between. A world that only the trapped souls seemed to know.

8 BY THE FIRE

By Sean Spinks
Investigator – Ghost Stories Inc.
Inspired by Spahn Ranch – Formerly the Primary Residence of Charles Manson and the Manson Family

Ryan could see the faint shimmer of the Hollywood lights in the distance, which told him he was nearly home. His brain had been teetering on the verge of shutting down for the last half hour. Too bad he still had another half hour left to drive. As his mind wandered, the canyon walls and trees became a blur that seemed to have no distinct shape at all. He hadn't seen another car for easily fifteen minutes. Not many people were out this time of night so far away from civilization.

His eyelids grew heavier as he struggled to keep them open. As he started to nod off, he caught a quick flash of something directly in his path.

Ryan jerked the wheel and came to a screeching halt. Adrenaline overpowered the fog of drowsiness that had clouded Ryan's head when he saw a young woman standing right in front of his car. The glow of the headlights lit the woman as if she were herself electrified, giving off her own light. Her hair draped over her face.

Ryan rushed out of the car without considering that there might be other cars traveling the winding, canyon road in the darkness of the night. His only thought was the woman who stood before him, unmoving.

"Are you okay?" he asked the woman.

She remained motionless, her face a mystery behind the cloak of the hair covering it.

"You and I almost made a terrible news headline. Why are you walking in the damn street out here?" Ryan asked, the realization that he could have killed the woman standing in front of him made his voice tight with tension.

Still, she did not respond. Ryan reached forward hesitantly and grabbed her shoulders.

"Do you need help?" he asked, his brow furrowed with concern.

The woman slowly cleared the hair from her eyes and replied with a simple nod of her head. Ryan walked her back to his car, opened the passenger door and slowly sat her down.

"Do you need a ride somewhere?" he asked.

The woman nodded again.

"Okay," Ryan replied, suddenly energized from the trauma. He quickly ran around the front of the car and settled behind the wheel. He regarded his odd passenger with a shake of his head.

"My name is Ryan. What's your name?" he asked.

"The family will be looking for me," she replied without emotion.

Ryan's left eyebrow raised with a look of slight confusion as he mouthed, "Okay . . ."

Slipping the car into drive, he asked, "Where can I take you?"

The woman pointed down the canyon road in the same direction Ryan had been driving. He hoped it wouldn't take too long to get rid of this strange, new friend he had acquired. As he drove down the twisting road, Ryan kept glancing at his passenger. Her clothing seemed handmade. She didn't seem to have any makeup on. She was wearing no jewelry. She couldn't be any more plain and nondescript. She was just a blank slate, as vacant as the expression on her face as she stared ahead through the windshield.

As his brain was playing detective, the woman raised her hand and pointed down a dirt road leading off the canyon highway. At this point Ryan was finished with his "good deed of the day" and just wanted to get home. He slowed the car and turned down the path.

They had driven less than a mile when the woman smiled and said quietly, "Here."

Ryan slowed the car and gazed around the long, overgrown, dirt road and saw only trees and rocks in every direction.

Who in their right mind would want to be dropped off in the middle of nowhere?

Ryan began to make a slow, wide turn on the narrow road to swing the car around to face the highway, hoping to drop his passenger off and drive away as quickly as possible. Something about the scenario made his skin spike with goose bumps. Before he rounded out the turn, his eyes caught a glimmer of light. He hadn't noticed it when he had driven in, but now he saw a small group of people sitting around a large campfire not more than seventy-five feet away.

"So this is the family, huh?" Ryan's voice was almost a whisper.

He turned to look at his passenger, but she was gone. He never heard the door open. It was as if she had just vanished from the car. He was confused, but chalked it up to his sleep-deprived brain blocking out the noise of the car door. Surely she had jumped out and run to her family, he thought. He finished making the U-turn in the narrow drive. Just then his conscience got the best of him, and he thought he should double check to make sure the girl had found her group. He begrudgingly got out of his car, stretched, and let out an audible yawn as he approached the fire.

"You must be the family," Ryan said to the group.

A short, bearded man slowly raised his eyes from the campfire to gaze at Ryan's face.

"That we are, my son," said the man. "Why don't you join us here by the fire? We're getting ready for a very special night."

The man stood up from the log he had been seated on and approached Ryan. As he got closer, his mouth never stopped moving.

NIGHT VISIONS

"You returned the girl to us. As the father, I cannot tell you how grateful I am. She's to be part of our special night." The odd little man smiled grimly in the moonlight. "The centerpiece, one might say."

"I really need to get going," said Ryan as he started backpedaling toward his car.

The man's face grew darker as he got further from the campfire. Shadows seemed to extend from his back as he got closer to Ryan. Ryan shook his head in disbelief as the man's eyes filled with a strange blackness. Ryan stumbled to the ground when he noticed the remaining members of the family stand up from the campfire and start moving toward him. Their arms and legs seemed to be stretched and were easily twice as long as any normal human's. As the family members got closer to Ryan, their human appearance melted into featureless shadow creatures that slinked toward him.

Ryan sprang back to his feet, as the man floated closer, his features still clear, but his eyes as black as tar, and whispered, "Now you're part of the family too. Join us by the fire, my son."

Gasping for a breath, Ryan fumbled his way into his car and slammed the door behind him. The shadow creatures were right behind him. Their long, dark fingers clawed at the windows as Ryan's hands frantically flipped through keys trying to find the one that would start the car. The car shook wildly under the weight of the creatures as Ryan turned the key.

As the engine roared to life, the headlights kicked on and illuminated a massive blob of what looked like solid, black smoke. Slamming on the gas pedal, Ryan punched a hole through the inky blackness only to see it reform in his review mirror. For a brief moment, he felt relief as his car dashed down the dirt drive, until he glanced in his review mirror and saw the cloud of collective shadow figures re-form. The mass grew closer to Ryan's car in the red glow of his taillights as he neared the main highway.

NIGHT VISIONS

As the tires transitioned from dirt to pavement, a familiar flash appeared in the headlights. This time, it was the father standing in Ryan's path. Instead of stopping, Ryan pounded the gas pedal in an effort to flatten the man. At the moment of impact the car simply passed through and seemed to hit nothing. Ryan kept his knuckles gripped around the steering wheel and his foot on the gas pedal.

The dirt road and the horrific shadow creatures were soon well out of sight. Finally, Ryan could catch his breath. He glanced at his reflection in the mirror and grimaced at his own reflection – it was the pale, sweat-covered face of someone in shock. As he glanced in his review mirror, the canyon became illuminated by flashing police lights following his car.

Ryan slowed his car to a stop, and the officer approached the driver's door and shined his flashlight at Ryan.

"Sir? Are you okay?" the officer asked, startled by the pale, blank look on Ryan's face. "You look like Hell."

Ryan recounted his tale of the hitchhiker and her family. Even he thought it sounded crazy.

"I have no idea what happened to her," said Ryan. "She just vanished."

"Son," the officer said, "I don't know if you're trying to pull a prank or something."

"No, sir. Not at all," said Ryan interrupting the officer. Ryan instantly regretted saying anything. He wished he'd just kept his mouth shut and taken the speeding ticket.

Ryan was surprised when the officer started talking.

"It's been nearly fifty years, almost to the day, that a young lady was murdered down in that valley," the officer told him. He continued his story with a serious look on his face. "She was a drifter who was picked up by this group of crazies, they called themselves "The Family." Those crazy bastards used her as a human sacrifice. Days later a group of locals raided their farm and burned it to the ground. They never gave those lunatics a chance to get out. They all died in the fire."

Ryan's heart pounded in his chest, and his head began to spin as he listened to the officer speak.

"Look, boy, I don't know what you saw back there, but if I've ever come across someone who looked like they've seen a ghost, it'd be you." The officer pointed ahead of the car. "You've got another mile to the highway that takes you to the interstate. You get going, but keep your speed down. I'm gonna be tailing you to make sure you do."

"Th . . .thank you," Ryan stammered. His hands shook as he shifted his car into drive, and eased backed onto the highway. The headlights of the police car behind him gave him a little comfort, but even with that, he couldn't look back. Every shadow on the side of the road made his heart jump and the voice of the strange man who called himself the father seemed to echo in his mind.

"Now you're part of the family too. Join us by the fire, my son."

9 THE DUNGEON

By Joshua Sterling Bragg
Director / Investigator – Ghost Stories Ink
Inspired by a Poor Farm in Minnesota

PART I

My father is a minister, and coincidentally so is my mother's father; so it's no surprise I spent my entire life wandering around old churches and graveyards during the week when no one else was around. Sometimes I even found myself exploring an old barn, or wandering through the basement of an abandoned farm house. I always enjoyed the energy in those places. It was charged. Looking back, it must have been obvious that

NIGHT VISIONS

I would grow up to be an explorer; as I had been drawn to old buildings my entire life.

When I was in grade school my courage was impregnable. The church my dad served was massive, to say the least, and I would spend hours exploring it, often in the dark of night while my father sat through lengthy meetings about budgets and funerals. The sanctuary could seat close to a thousand people. It was one of those massive, old Pennsylvania churches with huge, wooden beams that seemed to be miles above your head. When I sat in a pew in the back, my father appeared miniaturized, so far away in the front, his booming voice echoing through the rafters.

But the sanctuary, albeit gigantic, was the smallest part of the church. The ground level of the rest of the building was filled with offices, the choir room, big board rooms, a library and a gymnasium. Down a few flights was another wing, still technically ground level because the church was built into a rolling hill, with a Sunday school classroom for each grade.

Out the back of the Sunday school wing was a massive graveyard that seemed to stretch endlessly up a big hill and beyond. It was a beautiful, but somber, backdrop to the immense building. I didn't go out there much. My dad didn't want me wandering around the graveyard as a kid because there were lots of visitors there paying respect to their deceased loved ones.

At the far end, just beyond a colonial, wooden fence, stood an old, stone building in a field that used to be the county poor farm. My dad and I once mowed the lawn together on a big tractor when the sexton was on vacation.

"Never come over here by yourself," my father told me. "Sad things happened here, and it doesn't belong to the church, so it's off limits."

He didn't have to say anything else to convince me to obey. I'd heard rumors of teenagers sneaking into the building and falling through boards. I'd even heard they died. I didn't want to die. After all, I was only ten, and I still had too much exploring to do.

I didn't spend much time messing around in the Sunday school classrooms. Yeah, they had some cool toys to play with and stuff to do, like make artwork, and that was fine, sometimes. Where I got my real kicks was in the basement. As large as this place was on ground level, it was equally huge underground, and a million times cooler. It was a maze of hallways and rooms. With few windows and no doors leading outside, even in broad daylight, it was pitch black beyond the stairwell.

On a good night, I'd spend at least twenty solid minutes jumping from couch to couch in the high-schoolers' room at the bottom of the stairs.

Not tonight, I thought as I walked past my usual first stop. I had something else in mind.

I walked through a series of rooms that were all connected to each other, then up a flight of stairs to a secret hallway. After a little more wandering, I came to a dark hallway that would have led me back to where I started. Instead, I decided to go into the great hall, and that's where the night got interesting.

PART II

The great hall was almost the same size as the sanctuary, and was directly under it. It had small, rectangular cellar windows at the top of the wall that let light in from above ground, so although it was dim with the lights off, you could see a little. At the back of the room was this door that the adults called "the dungeon".

Kids weren't allowed to go in the dungeon, not that any of us could muster up the courage, anyway. Almost every Sunday, kids would dare each other to go in when nobody was looking, but no one would ever do it. I had peeked in once when it was open, and it was dark and filthy. The whole building was waxed linoleum floors, white drop ceilings, and squeaky-clean, glossy-white painted walls, but not "the dungeon" – it was dirt brown. Almost as if it was carved out of the earth like a tomb.

NIGHT VISIONS

As I approached the door that night, with my heart beating in my throat, I felt panicked; yet somehow, beneath the veil of fear, I felt strong. I wanted to be the cool kid when the rumors spread. I wanted to tell everyone the legends of the dungeon and not just be a scared, little kid, like everyone else. So I moved forward, forcing myself to stand strong in front of the big, wooden door.

I will not be afraid. I will not be afraid. I will not be afraid, I repeated to myself. But I was very afraid.

The door was old, beat up and severely out of place. I looked around, taking in the great hall in all of its shiny, white glory. How could it be that in the hundreds of years that this building has been here, none of the caretakers, ministers, or congregation members had replaced the door or boarded it up, or even locked it? But none of that mattered; I wanted to be the hero.

With a deep breath, I grabbed the knob on the dungeon door and pulled it open. It reacted exactly the way you'd think a big, old door would: with a long, deep creek, as it slowly opened, shaking loose dirt into the cool breeze that was now biting at my face.

I shielded my eyes from the dust, and when it settled, giving into a small shiver, opened them again to see.

BLACK

All I could see was black.

at first.

As my eyes adjusted a bit, I could see a few inches into the dungeon. It was exactly as I had remembered it. The floors and walls were mustard-brown dirt, like you'd see in an archeological dig site. In fact, it was entirely possible they had been carved out of the earth by humans hundreds, if not thousands, of years ago. Okay, maybe not thousands, but I was ten, and at the time, it seemed like a logical thought.

The floor caught the light of the great hall behind me, but only in the middle, creating a narrow path. Closer to the walls, the light fell off as if there was no ground there at all. As if the path was hovering above the ground.

A levitating walkway.

About thirty feet in front of me, a string dangled from the ceiling.

A lightbulb!

That was exactly what I needed, so I inched forward. Careful to stay on the illuminated part of the path. It was so cold in the dungeon. And so dark. And there was a strange smell I couldn't quit put my finger on. It was almost like the fridge when something's starting to rot inside.

I inched further towards the little, white string – my safety pull, my life line. With each step, I became more and more afraid. I wondered why I was so scared. I had been through the entire basement a million times in pitch-black darkness, relying on only my sense of touch. So why was I panicking, as if something would pop out and eat me?

I was inches from the string, when the subtle breeze that had been nipping at my face from deep inside the dungeon started to pull back, and there was a strange noise behind me. I turned quickly towards the door, losing sight of the string that would bring me light, just in time to catch a glimpse of a shadowed figure standing just inside the dungeon, silhouetted by bright, white room as the door slammed shut behind it.

Part III

Why didn't I listen? Why did I have to be the hero?

But, why didn't matter. The fact was, I was locked in utter darkness inside a dungeon, twelve feet underground, where no one could hear my cries. The only question that truly mattered was the one more terrifying than any I had ever wondered.

Did I really see something standing in the doorway right before it shut?

In situations like these, the only way to move forward is to convince yourself otherwise. No matter how sure you are, unless you have some sort of doubt in your mind about what you saw, you are frozen like dog crap in the winter.

Thoughts rapid-fired through my mind. *How could someone be standing there? The church is empty. The session meeting tonight isn't for a few hours, and it'll be on the opposite side of the property. Adults turn on lights when they go through a building. That was too tall to be a kid. Unless I was down here longer than I thought, and Dad was playing a trick on me.*

I decided to call out, hoping it was him. "Daaad?"

Nothing.

"Daaaaaaad? Is that you?"

Nothing.

Okay, nothing's happened in the past minute, I thought. *I'll find the light.*

NIGHT VISIONS

Even if nothing was there, pulling the dangling string seemed like a safer bet then traveling towards my hallucination to open the door, especially since I had no idea what was on other side of this walkway. I slowly turned, being careful where I stepped, and reached up, into the darkness. I knew it was right there. I had just seen it. But I didn't feel anything. I swiped my hands around again and again, grasping for the string. The longer my back was turned to the door, the more afraid I became of being in the dark and the possibility that I was not alone.

Am I facing the wrong way? I wondered.

I turned back to where I thought the door had been, but there was no light coming in at all. With such an old, rickety door, I expected some light to seep through the cracks, but I turned in a complete circle, and there was no light anywhere.

Which way did I come in, and where the heck is that light string?

I felt another breeze, almost like the dungeon was exhaling again. It was as if I was inside the throat of an ice breathing dragon. Freezing air encapsulated my body, and I started to feel tired, which made no sense. I wondered if the dungeon was somehow trying to lull me to sleep.

My body feels heavy, I thought, completely perplexed by my sudden desire to lie down. *But I'm too scared to sleep here. What if I roll off the side? What if I die?*

I tried to push the thought out of my mind and focus on coming up with a plan of escape. I decided it would be safer to crawl on my hands and knees. That way I could feel if there was a drop-off on the floor without falling into it. I knew how far the door was, roughly, so if I didn't reach it and I didn't reach a wall or some sort of pit, then all I had to do was turn around.

So I crawled.

NIGHT VISIONS

After a few steps my hand came to an edge in the floor. Frightened, I quickly backed away, as if a claw was going to come out of the abyss and get me.

Decision time. Left or right?

The cold breeze blew again, ever so gently, from my right.

Yes, a clue! I remembered the breeze was coming from inside the dungeon, so I needed to turn away from the air to get to the door. *Genius!*

I had the feeling that I was going to cry. Not a bad cry, but like a proud-of-myself cry that I get when I do something I never thought I could.

I just solved the impossible problem of the cold, dark dungeon!

I turned left and crawled towards the door. I was excited; not only was I going to get out, but I was going to have quite a story for the other kids in Sunday school this weekend! I had to keep my wits and move very slowly so I didn't accidentally fall off the side. And right before I got to the door, I noticed something strange.

Out of nowhere, in the black void that was stretching infinitely in front of me, there was a movement. I knew there was a movement because slowly but surely, a little crack of light was coming back from underneath the door. As if something was moving out of the way; like a curtain being swept aside. And there was a little light that hurt to look at. The door was almost directly in front of me. As my eyes began to adjust, I froze on my hands and knees, terrified again of what was before me. Something really was there; it had been standing in front of the door the entire time.

I should have tried harder for the light string, I thought. I wanted to see. I was too afraid of the door to get any closer, and I had no idea where the thing was that had been in front of it.

How is everything getting worse? I wondered.

I whispered a little prayer. "I'm sorry God, I didn't mean to disobey the adults. Please don't let me die."

Then I imagined a response. At least, I think I did. My brain heard it, but my ears didn't. As the darkness slowly covered the crack in the door again, three stark words penetrated my brain like a hot bullet:

God's not here.

While my eyes were still adjusting to the small amount of light from the door, I turned to look again for the light string. A split second. THERE! There it was, dangling in the air twenty feet back, glowing as if the crack in the door was lighting it perfectly! This was my one and only chance to change the odds. I stood and sprinted towards the thin, white string that dangled in the air as the darkness around me grew. My eyes began to lose focus, and my feet began to lose balance.

Stay straight! Stay on the path! I thought with each footfall.

The room seemed to elongate in the darkness, and time slowed down. And just as everything went black, I snatched the string out of the air and pulled.

NIGHT VISIONS

Part IV

Click.

Amazing how a tiny click can be the difference between infinite blackness and beautiful, warm, safe light. Lucky for me the sexton kept fresh bulbs in the sockets down there. Suddenly, I was feeling very silly about being oh-so-very afraid.

It can't be too dangerous if adults come in here to change the lightbulbs, I reasoned.

I looked around. There was no one in the room with me, and everything looked normal. Well, as normal as it looked when I first opened the door. The walls were flat, yellowish dirt that ran only about six and a half feet high, topped by an aged wood ceiling. The floor was concrete, but it was covered in dirt from the walls. Just beyond the center of the room where I huddled, the smooth concrete dropped away to dark pits on either side, making the floor feel more like a walkway between hollow tombs waiting to swallow me whole.

I crept towards the pit on the left which was about three feet wide and deeper than I could see. They ran like twins on either side of the path for about ten yards. Horrible, dark things.

Don't get too close! I thought, but I wanted to look down. It would make me feel much better to know how deep they are.

I lowered myself onto my hands and knees and eased closer, careful to keep all of my weight anchored to the cold, hard concrete. Closer still. Black. Impossibly black. The falloff of the light was almost immediate.

It could be a few inches deep or a few miles. It was impossible to tell. So I spit into it.

Nothing.

I looked around the floor for a small pebble or something to toss down. Maybe if I could hear how deep it was, I wouldn't be so terrified.

Nothing.

NIGHT VISIONS

Then I remembered, I had a penny in my pocket. I laid on my stomach to approach the ledge and dropped the penny over the side, making a wish, just in case.

. . . .
. . . . .kaploop!

Wow. Apparently deep and filled with water.

Knowing this did not make me feel better. In fact, it made me dizzy. It made it impossible to stand. In that moment, the big dungeon became just a little room with deep, dark, deathly holes on either side – and suddenly it seemed to be spinning. The walls were closing in, and it was as if I was meant to fall into the pit. I was sure of it.

But which one? I wondered. *The room will decide! I can't move. What happens after I fall? How deep is the water? Will I die right away or float around and starve to death?*

Now it made sense why the adults didn't want us down here. They didn't want kids goofing around and falling into the terrifying pit of doom.

I tried to think about something calming. So I laid there for a moment thinking of dogs, puppies – everyone I'd ever seen. And the walls began to recede. The room stopped spinning. And once again I was just a kid in a room.

Still afraid to stand up, I eased back on my hands and knees to the middle of the floor. I crawled towards the door.

The scratchy floor hurt my hands and knees, but I was perfectly happy to bleed a little if it meant living past ten. All was going well as I scuttled towards the door, back towards the safe basement of the church, when a cold breeze snuck by my ear and the door slowly started to swing open.

And I was frozen again. Even if it was just a draft, I didn't like it.

I'd heard that door click shut earlier. So how could a breeze . . .?

I stopped myself. I'd had enough being scared for the night. The door was open now. A sign that I could leave. So I pressed on, forcing the questionable thoughts out of my mind.

((((SLAM))))

The door shut with a force that made me drop to my stomach. Then it slowly creaked open.

(((SLAM))))

There was no explanation for what was happening as I watched the door open and shut, open and shut, open and shut.

BANG! BANG!! BANG!!! BANG!!!!

Jumping to my feet, I ran deep into the dungeon – back into the darkness. Past the pits, to where the floor connected to the walls, and the ceiling got lower and lower and lower until I could feel my hair brush against them as I hurried onward. I ran, without turning back, pulling string after string, illuminating lightbulbs along the ceiling as I made my way deeper and deeper into the dungeon.

NIGHT VISIONS

Part V

I had no idea where I was. I ran until I couldn't hear the door slamming anymore – until I couldn't breathe anymore – until the stupid ceiling was so low and the walls were so tight that I was hunched over and couldn't go any further. I kept moving forward until I got to another door.

The dungeon didn't seem to really be a dungeon at all. Up to that point it had been just a long, crappy hallway. I had a decision to make. Open the door, or head back up the impossibly long hallway to the other door – the scary door.

"Damn," I said under my breath, a little cautious someone might hear me cursing.

Then a hopeful thought slipped into my mind. *If there's a cold wind coming from way down here causing the door at the other end to open and shut, then that must mean there is a way out back here!*

I remembered this from the adventure books my dad used to read me. If you get lost in a cave, deep underground, go towards where the breeze is coming from. Which is exactly what I did, and it led me to this door. So, I had to go through it.

I reached toward the engraved brass doorknob, slowly turned it to the left, and pushed. A cold gust of stale air smacked my cheeks as dust fell from the top of the doorframe. I coughed, wiping my eyes. It was dark in there. Darker than the hallway, and almost none of the light spilled in with the exception of a small pool on the floor.

Before completely entering the room, I thought to search for a light switch on the walls. Maybe this room would be different, since it seemed to be more of a room than a long, crappy hallway. Lifting my hand to the right of the door, I touched the inside wall.

My finger slipped into a hole and I immediately thought, *Spiders!*

I pulled my hand away fast. There was a bizarre texture to the wall. It was cold and smooth and swollen, but with jagged holes.

NIGHT VISIONS

I was just caught off guard. *There's nothing scary about some holes in a wall,* I thought, trying to reason with myself. So I reached back, running my hand slowly down the wall, exploring its texture and searching for a switch. It was made of round pieces, almost like a warped tile or a large stone you'd find smoothed out at the bottom of a riverbed, but it had all kinds of holes in it. Two big holes, then a triangle hole and then tickticktick bunch of little bumps. Then repeat. Big round curve, two big holes, triangle hole, tickticktick bunch of little bumps. Repeat.

I reasoned that must be some sort of decorative tile from a long time ago, and refocused my thoughts on finding a light. There was no way a wall like that was going to have a switch. It had to be another pull string. I stepped forward into the dwindling light from the hall, reaching my hands into the air like a zombie, looking for a light string.

My eyes were adjusting, but not very well. The last light of the hallway had stopped several feet from the door. I kept moving forward, hands searching the air as I began to feel the room change around me. The walls and the ceiling didn't feel close any more. In fact they didn't feel like they were there at all.

Another cold wind, and I heard the door slowly creak shut behind me.

"Damn."

I wasn't turning back. I had decided approaching doors that close on their own was not a great plan. I kept my cool and shuffled on in perfect darkness.

Seconds felt like hours as I stumbled forward in the dark. Then my hand touched something scratchy. It startled me. I wasn't sure what it was, but I told myself not to freak out, and gave it another touch. To my relief, I found a swinging knot of twine dangling from the ceiling.

Click. Light.

Awesome! Awesome light! And what's in front of me? I wondered.

NIGHT VISIONS

Stairs! Lots and lots of stairs, with a big metal door at the top, like a cellar door.

It's not just a door. It's salvation! I thought, my heart racing with relief.

Part of me wanted to run to it, but I needed to turn around to see the massive room I had just passed though. I'd spend the rest of my life thinking about this place, and I wanted to know what the weird, rounded tiles looked like with the big, round curve, and the two large holes, and the triangle hole and the tickticktickticktick bunch little bumps. So I turned around, and my jaw dropped. I felt as if I had been punched in the stomach, and the air had been knocked out of me.

My butt slammed onto the bottom step, as I stared into the dimly lit room at the walls, which to my horror were lined with human skulls.

Vile.

    Awful.

        Terrifying.

            And strangely beautiful...

I didn't spend much time soaking it in. As soon as my body would let me, as soon as I replenished my air, I turned and climbed with amazing speed up the long stairway. I'd had enough, and nothing was going to keep me down there. I don't know if it was just my imagination running wild, or the mental suggestion of all those skulls smiling at me with their tikticktiktick little bumps, but I felt the cold wind at my back as if to suggest the way out was back into the dungeon. Like something wanted me to turn and see it. But I refused to look back. Instead, I climbed.

Exhausted, I finally reached the door. With my legs giving out and my lungs burning with the hot stink of surrounding death, with all my remaining little boy strength, I threw it open.

Yes! Freedom! At last!

Part VI

With my hands on my knees, my chest heaved as I sucked in rapid gulps of air. I expected to inhale the fresh, crisp air of the countryside. Instead the air was dank and filled with old basement smell, which was better than the smell of a thousand deaths I had been soaking in. I hadn't found a doorway outside, but seemed to still be underground. As I inhaled, I recognized the smell from the log cabins we would wander through at Valley Forge Park during the summertime, the cabins had been there since the revolutionary war. This place, like the cabins, stank from centuries of humans living and dying in these walls. The wood soaked it in and made it eternal; this smell was historic.

There was a faint glow coming from above, but by any stretch of the imagination, I was not outdoors as hoped. Pale-blue moonlight stretched like elderly fingers through gaps in the ceiling that alternated from perfectly uniform to warped. My first thought was how exceptionally low the ceiling was.

My dad wouldn't be able to stand in here, I thought. *Where am I?*

NIGHT VISIONS

A dark rumble came from the door behind me. A jolt of electric fright shot through me as I jumped, smacking my head against what I now recognized as floorboards. I didn't remember there being any other buildings on the church property.

((((SLAM))))

The cold, evil air sucked the door closed behind me, and as I searched its rusty surface for a handle, a piercing thought settled into my brain. *It's too late to turn back.*

Whatever put those words into my mind was right. The only way to go was forward. I shivered a little, closing my eyes as if the darkness might warm me or at least give me an idea of what to do next. Closing my eyes felt good – very good. I wanted to keep them closed, but I couldn't. Although I was exhausted and ready to sleep, the more I kept my eyes close, the more I felt like I might not be alone.

There was a heaviness growing in the room. It wasn't the heaviness of being drowsy or standing for too long. I felt heat on the back of my neck, as if someone was standing too close, staring at me, waiting for me to turn, open my eyes and see them. I knew I had to open my eyes, but now I wasn't sure I could.

What if whatever chased me down here wanted me to end up in this place all along? What if the shadow was here waiting to swallow me whole? I had no plan of escape, no options.

I tried to calm myself.

Taking a deep breath of stale air, I opened my eyes, fully intending to prove there was nothing there, and then I saw him.

Part VII

I began to tremble from the deepest catacombs within me. The temperature lowered like water being siphoned from a basin, and I could feel my marrow hardening inside my bones. I opened my mouth to scream, but only a jagged whimper climbed out. I stared at him helplessly, unsure what to do next.

Timothy.

The name ripped into my brain and stuck like an arrow. Timothy. What a strangely unassuming name for what I was looking at.

Timothy was short like me, but that was where the similarities ended. His skin was midnight blue, which made him impossible to see in the shadows, but where the ladyfingers of light danced across his body, I could see the almost oil-stained smoothness of his skin. He stood upright, naked and completely hairless. His bald head sloped backwards and was slightly bigger, if not swollen, in the back. His eyes were small and perfectly white; no pupil; no iris.

I wondered if he could see me. I wondered if he thought I was strange looking, too. Although his mouth didn't look hard, it was shaped like a beak, but not like a bird; more like a turtle. His head sat on his shoulders with no sign of a neck. His right arm was short and rested on his inflated pot-belly, and the other was long hanging off to his left where his fingers danced gently on his bare thigh. The last thing I noticed was his backwards knees, bent and ready to run like a baby ostrich.

Timothy's eyes blinked sideways at me, and for a split second he was invisible. My dad always taught me to accept people who were different, and with a name like Timothy, well, he had to be an okay guy, right?

"Are you Timothy?"

He nodded.

"Do you live here?"

He nodded again. I was proud of myself.

"What is this place?"

Timothy gestured with his long arm for me to follow him, then turned and crept forward on his ever-squatting legs. He wasn't as scary when he walked. In fact, he was almost funny. Because of the bend in his legs, his upper body didn't move when he walked, it just sort of floated. I imagined Timothy and myself trick-or-treating together.

All he needed was a white sheet, and he would be the most convincing ghost ever! It would look exactly like he was hovering over the ground! I liked the thought of this and tried my best to follow him without bobbing up and down like a normal human.

We crossed the basement which was filled with old, torn mattresses, their straw stuffing bled out onto the floor. The hay didn't make a sound under Timothy's feet, but it crunched like bones under my high tops. He led me to a staircase and waved for me to go up first.

I made my way to the first step, placed both hands on the floor-ceiling above me and pushed. Despite how heavy it was, I managed to make it move.

A trap door! I thought as I moved up to the next step. Squatting, I pushed with all of my might, stood tall, shoved the secret floorboard door open and climbed into a kitchen. At least I assumed it was a kitchen. There was no fridge or microwave, but there was a sink. My parents didn't have a microwave either, so it didn't seem too strange. A microwave doesn't define you, it's just makes it easier to make popcorn.

Timothy came up behind me, silently. Light pooled like mystic puddles beneath the boarded up windows and bounced gently into the room. Timothy made sure to stick to the shadows.

"You're not safe here. Little boys aren't supposed to wander about such places." Timothy told me through his thoughts.

Somehow, it didn't seem strange that he was talking to my brain, without ever speaking words.

"We need to keep moving before he gets here."

"Who's he?" I replied wordlessly.

"The one who led you here. The one in the shadows."

"How do you know he'll find us here?" I asked.

Timothy didn't respond right away, which made me nervous. But when Timothy finally spoke I understood why he was communicating in thoughts, and why we needed to leave this place right away.

"*He lives here.*"

Part VIII

I ran for the front door, only there was no way out. It was boarded up with two by fours.

"There's no way out!" I cried out. "I can't go back the way I came I just can't!"

As if on cue, an awful, musty breeze came from the floorboards, twisting up my pant legs like a snake.

"*That way is no longer safe. He sealed it,*" Timothy warned.

"Who is the man in the shadows? Why is he here?"

"*He's a very bad man. He built this place.*"

"Where are we?"

"*The poor farm.*"

Guilt spread like a sickness inside me. I knew I wasn't supposed to be in here. My father warned me, but I didn't listen. I knew I was in trouble, but I had so many questions. I turned, looking at the open room behind me as another cold breeze ruffled my shirt and tickled my spine. As I explored the room our thoughts swam back and forth like Chinese fighting fish.

"Timothy, do you live here?"

"Yes."

"Were you born here?"

"Yes."

"Do your parents live here?"

"Not anymore. My mother did, my father left when I was born."

"How old are you?"

"I'm ten." His next thought came at me urgently. *"We need to leave."*

But I wanted to know more. "Where is your Mother?"

"In the woods."

"What is she doing there?"

"He put her there. He'll put you there too." His thoughts shot at me rapidly. Even without speaking them, I could sense his fear.

"What do you mean he . . .?"

"We need to go right now!" Timothy cut my thought off before I could get it all out.

I wanted an answer. Just as I turned to speak out loud to Timothy, I noticed an empty, black form growing behind him.

"Timothy, run!" I screamed, scaring the bats awake in the rafters.

The room became alive with flying rodents. Ten, twenty, a hundred bats, swarmed every which way. I shielded my face as they flew by, blurring together in a solid wall of movement. Through them, I watched as Timothy was swallowed by the nothingness that had formed behind him. I wondered if it was the man from the shadows.

NIGHT VISIONS

The bats changed their formation. Instead of flying every which way, they were now flying a perfect circle around me. Moonlight shone through their cracks like a projector. Amidst the slight differences in their coloration, I began to see images. Moving bodies. People. The walls of the old rundown farm house started to look new, as if they had been freshly painted. A little boy my age and height, ran by. Although he looked different, he reminded me of . . ..

"Timothy!" A woman said, "Where have you been?"

The bats shifted, and so did the room. An older man, with a black hat held a cane over Timothy, who was bent over a bench.

"You little wretch! This'll teach you to wander off and skip out on your work!"

The cane came down, missing its mark, and cracked across the back of Timothy's knees. He screamed in pain as the bats shifted, and in an instant we were inside a bedroom where Timothy laid in bed, thin and weak with casts on both of his legs. The man in the hat stood at the foot of his bed.

"Timothy, your mother is dead. She'll be buried with the rest of them," the man said, his voice emotionless.

Timothy began to cry.

"I'm very sorry you didn't get to see her," the man continued coldly. "Maybe if you had been obedient and done your work like all the other boys and girls around here, you would have been able to get out of bed and be at her side. That was very selfish of you. I hope you've learned your lesson." He tapped his cane a little too hard on Timothy's cast, causing him to whimper like a hurt animal.

The bats swelled again, and I saw Timothy working in a field. He looked over his shoulder at the bad man who stood in the distance; the butt of his rifle came down on the head of a woman. Frightened by what he saw, Timothy ran towards the woods, never looking back. A shot rang out like a thunderclap just before Timothy dropped.

In a flash, Timothy was gone. But he wasn't buried. As the bats swelled and shifted around me one last time, I saw the bad man standing over a fire pit, while many others sat around him and watched, their faces somber and stained with tears.

"Timothy didn't like to listen. Timothy didn't like to work. Well neither do I, but I do it! Do you know why? Because this is what happens when you don't listen and don't do your work," the man said, stirring the fire, his lips curled in a thin sneer. "You have all been sent here for a reason. Because the rest of America doesn't want you! They're disgusted by you, so they sent you to me! You don't get the privilege of living here if you don't do your goddamn work! Those are the rules! I didn't make them up, your country did. So show some respect for the institution that is giving you food and giving you shelter, and do your damn work so this doesn't need to happen again!"

The bats exploded in every direction around the room, showing years of pain and suffering all at once. People dying of sickness, of starvation, and at the hand of the bad man. Their bodies were taken deep into the woods and gutted like deer. Their flesh parts were buried all in the same place. No marker; just out there to be forgotten. Their bones were taken beneath the floorboards of the poor house and boiled in bleach. In a flash, I saw the man take the bones to the tunnels and build his catacombs. Building more with each fresh kill.

In a few seconds, I saw fifty years pass. I watched the man's rise and fall. I saw him place the barrel of his shotgun into his mouth and pull the trigger. Brains flew out the back of his head, but instead of spraying the walls, they slowed down, turning to black. They became like a satin fabric, all joining together and flowing to the floor like a cape. Darkness shrouded his body like ink from an octopus as he transformed from his despicable human form into an impossibly black mass – a void in existence.

NIGHT VISIONS

Years passed. No matter how hard the man's spirit tried to leave, he was stuck in this place. I saw flashes of him trying to lure people into his basement, where perhaps he could add to his collection. I also saw Timothy's spirit; always one step ahead of the shadow the man had become, always finding ways to warn people before it was too late. If the man was a demon, Timothy was an angel.

Suddenly, the bats came in close, blacking out the images – blacking out the room altogether. They were too close and I fell to the ground, covering my eyes. I landed on something soft. The air around me grew colder and the sound of the bats flapping began to fall away.

I opened my eyes to find myself lying on the grass outside the old poor house. Crickets were singing. Stars were shining and the house, that just moments before had been alive with horror, was silent. I let out a sigh, tossed my hands loosely into the grass on either side of my head, and let my body relax for a second as I caught my breath.

Thank you Timothy, I thought. I didn't know how, but I knew he saved me. I sprang to my feet, wanting to be as far away from that damned house as possible, and ran through the graveyard and down the hill, never slowing my pace until I stood at the backdoor of the church.

Finding the door locked, I had to pound on the window of my dad's meeting to get in. Of course, I got a lecture about going outside at night and playing in the graveyard. I took it as a happy alternative to explaining what had actually occurred in the dungeon and beyond in the forbidden poor house, which I never spoke of again.

Except to my friends in Sunday school.

GHOST STORIES INK

Jessica Freeburg's fascination with history and the paranormal fuels many of her creative works. As the founder of Ghost Stories Ink, she has performed paranormal investigations at a variety of reportedly haunted locations. *LIVING IN SHADO*WS: BOOK One of THE SHADOWS SERIES is her debut novel. Her second book, a middle grade nonfiction about the Holocaust will be released in the fall of 2016. She serves on the editorial staff of *FATE Magazine* and is a correspondent for the popular paranormal radio program *Darkness Radio*. Additionally, she's the Assistant Regional Advisor for the Society of Children's Book Writers and Illustrators of Minnesota. To learn more about Jessica, go to www.jessicafreeburg.com.

A Graduate of the Minneapolis College of Art and Design, **Shawn McCann** is a multi-media, multi-disciplinary artist whose work includes 3D street painting, murals, fine art, children's books, installation art, and commercial illustration. His work has won numerous awards and is held in private and public collections. He has been featured twice at the *LA Times* Festival of Books as a featured illustrator on the children's stage. Shawn has also worked on two National Endowment for the Arts Grant and a number of Minnesota State Legacy grant projects. Learn more about Shawn at www.shawnmccann.com.

Having recently escaped his shallow grave, **Sean Spinks** has been hard at work giving life to movie and comic book poster art under the guise of Horrorizons (on Facebook). His art has been featured in *Invest Comics Deadly Tales: One and Done*, the *Terror of Dracula* promotional web comic series and as the cover of the horror anthology, *Death Awaits,* by Harren Press. His art and writing is featured in the horror anthology, *Bad Taste: Volume 1.* He has a lovely bride and four little monsters at home.

Joshua Sterling Bragg is the owner and co-founder of an independent Brooklyn-based production company, that produces cinematography and post production for everything from corporate videos to music videos to feature films; he's also a writer. Although most of his stories have been published in video format (youtube.com/HauntingSeason), in 2014 he was published for the first time in the anthology *DEATH AWAITS* (Harren Press, 2014). His story, "Paul's Rose," is currently being converted to a feature film which he hopes to film in late 2016. For updates on Joshua's latest projects visit JoshuaSterlingBragg.com.

Natalie Fowler has been fascinated by ghost stories ever since she was a little girl, but she always wanted to know more about the ghost. Now, she writes her own ghost stories and she makes sure to give the ghosts a voice. Her paranormal mystery series is set in St. Paul, Minnesota. Once a practicing attorney, now Natalie does freelance editorial work. She also works as a staff editor at *FATE Magazine* and *Galde Press*. Natalie is a research geek, and could easily spend hours in the library with dusty old books. A member of Ghost Stories Ink, she is happy to fulfill any of the team's research needs. Natalie is currently working on a middle grade urban fantasy, so that her kids can finally read something she writes. Learn more about Natalie at www.nataliefowler.com.

FRIENDS OF GHOST STORIES INK

Jay Asher's debut teen novel, *THIRTEEN REASONS WHY*, was a #1 New York Times bestseller and has been performed on stage in the U.S. and Germany. His second teen novel, *THE FUTURE OF US*, was coauthored with Carolyn Mackler. His novels have been sold in over thirty foreign languages.

Sammy Sarzoza is an award winning screenwriter, grant finalist, working commercial producer/director, and seasoned live sports videographer. He's the owner and operator of Sarzoza Productions LLC, a video production company that has two divisions: Kitbash Ltd, which produces and develops creative media, and Stemless Media, a commercial production company. Sammy recently completed two narrative short films, while developing his first feature. In addition, he continues to develop his transmedia project, GeekyPheebs.com He was born in Saint Paul, MN; he currently resides in Los Angeles, CA.

RETREAT ANTHOLOGY CONTEST WINNERS

L. W. Edwards lives along the Minnesota River with her husband enjoying her gardens and the wildlife of Minnesota. She has enjoyed a career in Medical Devices for many years where she's been privileged to work with some of Americans finest servicemen. Her curiosity of the paranormal and cold cases have lead her on many intriguing adventures.

Crystal Brutlag is a young adult novelist and lifestyle blogger living in Minneapolis. She spends her days chatting with children at an elementary school, but at night you'll find her concocting fanciful stories or updating her lifestyle blog. She loves her dog to the moon and back; she firmly believes in dancing in the rain.